G R JORDAN

The Academy for Murder

A Highlands and Islands Detective Thriller #48

First edition

ISBN (print): 978-1-917497-37-4
ISBN (digital): 978-1-917497-36-7

This book was professionally typeset on Reedsy.
Find out more at reedsy.com

You just have to take a deep breath, relax and let the game come to you.

A J GREEN

Contents

Foreword

The events of this book, while based around real and also fictitious locations around the UK, are entirely fictional and all characters do not represent any living or deceased person. All companies are fictitious representations and locations have been modified for the purposes of the story. I know of no academy at Applecross. This novel is best read within a time-tabled curriculum with some detention for added focus and better results.

Acknowledgments

To Ken, Jean, Colin, Evelyn, John and Rosemary for your work in bringing this novel to completion, your time and effort is deeply appreciated.

Books by G R Jordan

The Highlands and Islands Detective series (Crime)

1. Water's Edge
2. The Bothy
3. The Horror Weekend
4. The Small Ferry
5. Dead at Third Man
6. The Pirate Club
7. A Personal Agenda
8. A Just Punishment
9. The Numerous Deaths of Santa Claus
10. Our Gated Community
11. The Satchel
12. Culhwch Alpha
13. Fair Market Value
14. The Coach Bomber
15. The Culling at Singing Sands
16. Where Justice Fails
17. The Cortado Club
18. Cleared to Die
19. Man Overboard!
20. Antisocial Behaviour
21. Rogues' Gallery
22. The Death of Macleod - Inferno Book 1

Kirsten Stewart Thrillers (Thriller)

1. A Shot at Democracy
2. The Hunted Child
3. The Express Wishes of Mr MacIver
4. The Nationalist Express
5. The Hunt for 'Red Anna'
6. The Execution of Celebrity
7. The Man Everyone Wanted
8. Busman's Holiday
9. A Personal Favour
10. Infiltrator
11. Implosion
12. Traitor

Jac Moonshine Thrillers

1. Jac's Revenge
2. Jac for the People
3. Jac the Pariah

Siobhan Duffy Mysteries

1. A Giant Killing
2. Death of the Witch
3. The Bloodied Hands
4. A Hermit's Death

The Contessa Munroe Mysteries (Cozy Mystery)

1. Corpse Reviver
2. Frostbite
3. Cobra's Fang

The Patrick Smythe Series (Crime)

1. The Disappearance of Russell Hadleigh
2. The Graves of Calgary Bay
3. The Fairy Pools Gathering

Austerley & Kirkgordon Series (Fantasy)

1. Crescendo!
2. The Darkness at Dillingham
3. Dagon's Revenge
4. Ship of Doom

Supernatural and Elder Threat Assessment Agency (SETAA) Series (Fantasy)

1. Scarlett O'Meara: Beastmaster

Island Adventures Series (Cosy Fantasy Adventure)

1. Surface Tensions

Dark Wen Series (Horror Fantasy)

Chapter 01

L ife was simple. The alarm went and Donnie got up. After all, Donnie had a job to do. He walked across his bedroom, pulled back the curtains, and looked out on a darkened landscape. Donnie didn't ponder it. He merely turned, walked through to a small bathroom, undressed, and stepped in the shower. Donnie didn't think of much as he washed himself down, scrubbed his hair, and then stood there rinsing off. Once that was done, he simply switched off the shower, stepped out, grabbed his towel, and dried himself. After dressing, Donnie made himself breakfast. That was the way of things. Get up, shower, breakfast. Once breakfast was done, and the dishes were washed and put away to one side, the day would begin proper, for Donnie had a job to do.

Donnie was a janitor. As much as Donnie didn't think of much when he was eating his scrambled eggs for breakfast, there was a sense of pride that reared up when his mind turned to the day ahead. As a janitor, he would open up the school, get everything ready for the staff and the young women who were part of the Applecross Academy for the Gifted. It was an all-girls school, catering for those aged sixteen and up. But for Donnie, that was irrelevant. This was simply his job. And in the main, the students were pleasant to him. The staff also said hello, although there were one or two who didn't really speak to him. That didn't bother Donnie. Donnie didn't need to speak to people either. He just needed to do his job. And his job today was to open up.

There was a coolness to the air as Donnie left his own on-site accommodation and walked over to the enormous gates of the driveway up to the school. He closed them every night and then opened them in the morning. No one else had a key except for the headmistress. And anyway, everyone was back in before Donnie closed up. So, there was no reason for anybody else to have a key. Donnie was there. And if they were going to be out very late, Donnie would organise a key for them. He would also detail to them what was to be done with that key and how to use it. Sometimes he thought they didn't appreciate that.

The grounds of the school were significant, and it would take Donnie a good half an hour to open everything up. There were the accommodation blocks, but he would avoid those, for the students would be rising, and breakfasting. They could open up their accommodation from the inside. He avoided the accommodation in the early morning. Sometimes, he had jobs inside the accommodation—items to fix, leaky taps, showers that were blocked—but he never went over too early to do those jobs. And he always had large signs advising people when he was working.

Instead, Donnie made his way over to what was the school part of the grounds. There were a good three hundred girls present at the school. Although the headmistress never liked to call them girls. She always called them young women. Donnie wasn't quite sure what the difference was, but he liked the headmistress. Miss Mackie—Miss Georgie Mackie as she announced herself—was kind to Donnie. In truth, he did everything she asked. He would run errands if need be. Life for Donnie was based at the school, and the good functioning of the school helped Donnie to be happy. He never had a holiday, for he didn't need one. He just liked routine.

Donnie approached the main building, what was termed the school on site. He opened the front doors after climbing the steps, and then stepped inside, switching on several lights. They hadn't got around to putting the automatic lights in yet, but that didn't bother Donnie. He enjoyed going through the place, switching on the lights at the start of the day and switching them off at the end. He strolled down corridors, illuminating the place, opening up doors that led to classrooms, the music suite, the mathematics department, English and art, too.

There he did pause briefly, looking at some new artwork that had been placed up on the wall of the classroom. He liked art. He liked music too, but at this time of the day no one was in the music suite, so there was no music to listen to. During the afternoon, he might pause, but never at the window of the classroom, always outside in the corridor listening. He didn't need to see them play. If he heard them, that was more than enough, for some of them were good. Talented. Much more than Donnie. He'd never been able to play an instrument.

Donnie continued towards the gymnasium. Mr Kershaw ran the gymnasium, one of the few male teachers on site. He was younger than Donnie, tall and strong with short-cut hair. He always joked with Donnie. Although Donnie was never sure what the joke was. Mr Kershaw was someone Donnie avoided as conversations always got awkward.

Donnie opened the sports hall office and switched on the lights. Then he went through and switched on the changing rooms' lights. Next, the double doors that led to the large hall to bring out whatever had been put away the night before. Donnie would pull out the ropes and frameworks, but as he looked inside, he was a little bemused. There was clothing all over the floor.

Donnie walked in and picked up some of the clothing. There was what looked like a woman's blouse. There was a man's shirt, a man's trousers, a man's underpants. *Why would you leave your underpants here?* thought Donnie. *What are they wearing now?* He looked on the floor. Donnie gasped for a minute and turned away. Then he turned back.

Yes, it was. It was women's underwear. A top set and a bottom set. Donnie was confused. He walked around the hall, looked into some of the side rooms, but there was no one there. Just this scattering of clothes across the gymnasium floor.

Donnie exited the hall and made for his janitor's closet, where he unravelled a black bin bag. He hurriedly brought it and a set of gloves back to the gymnasium, put the gloves on, and then picked up all the clothes, gingerly dropping them into the black bag. Wrapping the black bag up, he took it back to his janitor's office, where he labelled it, putting down the date and the time that he'd found it. He then took off the gloves and smiled.

That was out of the way. He looked at the clock on the wall. He'd need to get moving. This had put him back somewhat, and he needed to make sure everything was open. Usually, one of the first people to arrive would be the headmistress, and Donnie knew he had to get there quickly. But he would always open the science department before he got to the headmistress's office.

Donnie sped round the science department as quickly as he could. Never running, since you did not run at the school. Not unless you were on the sports pitch, or you were in the gymnasium. It was a rule, and Donnie had heard it many times. And Donnie followed rules. Having illuminated the science department, Donnie hurried along the administration corridors, opening those up before arriving at the headmistress's office.

As he went to walk up the corridor to it, Donnie stopped. There was light coming from under the door. The door itself was opaque, with no windows. But at this time of the morning, and with the darkness outside, light spilled out into the hallway. As Donnie hadn't illuminated the hall yet, it was easily evident.

Donnie switched on the hall light and approached the door. He knocked it several times and then stood, waiting patiently. There was no movement. Nothing from inside. That was strange. It was also strange that Miss Mackie would be in there this early. She should be another ten minutes. Donnie knocked again.

Was something up? He wondered. *What could be up? The headmistress wouldn't be in her office at this time. I always beat her to it.* Donnie knocked a third time, and when there was no answer, he tried the handle. The doorknob turned easily, and Donnie gingerly pushed the door open a fraction.

'Miss Mackie? Sorry to bother you, but the lights were on. Miss Mackie, you there?'

Donnie stood for a few moments, but there was no answer. Eventually, he decided he would need to make sure everything was okay. He knocked again on the door, and then pushed it open wide, stepping quickly inside and closing the door behind him, as if its being open would be an affront. He turned around from the door, looked over towards Miss Mackie's desk, and froze.

Donnie was accustomed to unpleasant sights. He had worked in a slaughterhouse and had seen men who could be tender with animals that they then put to death, for that was their job. He had seen his mother die on the roadside as they tried to save her; her body mangled, having been hit by several cars. Donnie wasn't squeamish. Blood was blood. Gore was gore. It was just what was inside you. These things didn't faze Donnie. But Donnie was fazed right now.

The headmistress's desk had old papers shoved off it. There were only two things on the headmistress's desk. One was a male mannequin. The other was the headmistress.

For a moment, Donnie struggled to understand whether she was alive or whether she was dead. The mannequin was lying on its back on the desk. For some reason, Miss Mackie was atop the mannequin, straddling it. She wasn't moving, though, as still as the mannequin beneath her. She also was wearing no clothes. The mannequin was undressed, too.

To Donnie, the scene was incomprehensible. *What was she doing with a mannequin? Why has she decided to take her clothes off?* Her hands were up behind her head, and Donnie just looked on in bemusement. He then turned, because on her whiteboard at the side of the office, somebody had drawn a word. Drawn, for they were large, chunky letters that had been coloured in.

It was a word he didn't recognise. It began with an S, then an L, a U, and ended with a T. There was one of those exclamation marks as well. The thing you wrote when you wanted to make it look as if somebody had shouted. Donnie's writing wasn't great, but he wasn't simple. He understood things, and he understood that whatever that word was, it was intended to be shouted. He turned and walked over to Miss Mackie.

'Miss Mackie, are you okay?' asked Donnie. He still wasn't sure whether she was alive or dead. Her eyes were open, but she didn't seem to register him. He waved a hand in front of her face. But again, nothing. Most people would have been squeamish to touch what could be a dead body. But from Donnie's point of view, if he didn't touch it, how would he know?

He put a hand on Miss Mackie's shoulder and shook her. 'Miss Mackie, are you there? Are you okay? We should get something on you,' said Donnie.

He shook her again, but there was no movement from Miss Mackie. He remembered there being no movement that fateful day from their pet dog. It was a long time ago, and the dog had simply died in the night, of old age. Donnie had felt sad when he'd found out. But before that, he had come across the dog who'd been lying there. A dog that would have jumped up at the approach of anyone. And Donnie had shaken the dog to see if it was okay.

He now shook Miss Mackie in exactly the same way and, like his dog, she didn't move. More than that, she seemed to be stuck in this position. Her arms didn't flinch. Locked. Donnie didn't know what to do. He turned for a moment, looking back to the door. And then marched across, opened it, and stepped outside. He locked the office.

Quickly, he made his way over to the accommodation area, where each of the teachers had their own place to stay. One of the largest was for Mrs Fotheringham-Smythe. She was the deputy headmistress. Whenever Donnie came across a problem, he would ask Miss Mackie, and if she wasn't there, he would approach Mrs Fotheringham-Smythe. She was older than Miss Mackie, and she was very matter of fact, but that suited Donnie.

Donnie approached her door and rang the doorbell. A few moments later, the door opened with Miss Mackie in a sensible dressing gown.

'Donnie? What's the matter, Donnie?'

'I've just been to the office of Miss Mackie.'

'And she's there?' There was silence for a moment. And then Mrs Fotheringham-Smythe said, 'Is everything okay, Donnie?'

Donnie shook his head. 'She's like my dog,' he said. 'She's gone like my dog.'

Chapter 02

Detective Chief Inspector Seoras Macleod sat in the passenger seat of the police car as it raced across the west of Scotland. Applecross was the destination. But Macleod had been in Thurso at a conference. It wasn't a conference he particularly wanted to go to, and he was glad to have left it. It was about budgeting. However, Macleod was never one to want someone to pass on, just so he could be called away on a job. Accordingly, he felt slightly guilty about being glad to be out of that conference.

The police officer beside him was saying very little, though every now and again he would glance at Macleod. Clearly, the officer knew who Macleod was. Macleod had said, 'Call me Seoras,' but the man never had. He'd said 'sir' quite a lot, or 'inspector.' Macleod was used to that. It was always the way, wasn't it? They introduced a new idea that we all have to talk to each other on a first-name basis. You try to get on with it, and people don't want to call you by your first name. Macleod wondered whether he intimidated people. Maybe they didn't want to be on that level with him. Well, he couldn't do anything about that.

The road ahead of him wound this way and that, and

Macleod thought of Jane back at home. Too often, he was called away. It used to be fine when he was on his own. After all, what else was he going to do? But Jane made things difficult. Not because she complained, but because, well, he should be there. He should spend some time with her. He shouldn't be away all the time. She'd given up a lot to come and be with him. He needed to pay that back.

But it was more than that, he realised. He was actually growing tired of it, something he never thought would happen. Police work had been his life. Now, he'd seen little Ian John born, Hope's first child. Hope McGrath had been his partner on the police force. They'd worked alongside each other, and the two would have raced off to any case. But now, Hope had a family, something Macleod had never managed.

No, that wasn't true. He had a family. Jane was his partner. She was family. He needed to make time for family. But the patch was so big, and now he was off to Applecross. Surely it should have been Glasgow's to handle, but they were busy at the moment with something else. They were always busy. And he wasn't?

After all, Hope was off on maternity. He was running three departments, albeit they weren't flat out at the moment. The Arts Department could practically run itself with Clarissa. Emmett was more than capable on the cold case side. Macleod was just covering Hope at the inspector level on the murder squad.

As the police car pulled in through the enormous gates of Applecross Academy for the Gifted, Macleod felt something different. Normally, he'd have been buzzing, racing to get in here. The case would be on. A hunt to be mastered. Not that he was dreading going in. Not that he was fed up with it. It just wasn't the way it used to be.

The police car wound up the long driveway after passing through a police cordon, towards some large buildings on the grounds. Once there, Macleod was waved through on showing his credentials to a very apologetic officer manning the entrance. Macleod thanked the officer driving the car for the lift and was then met by a face he knew well.

Detective Sergeant Alan Ross had raced straight down from Inverness to take charge of the scene.

'Ross, what's happening?'

'Good afternoon, sir,' said Ross. 'I hope you've had a pleasant journey down. We've cordoned off the area where the body was found. I'll take you through to have a look at that in a moment. Jona's in there. She'll be able to advise you a little more. It's the headmistress of the school. Thirty-year-old. Female.'

'The headmistress? Who are you talking to then regarding the school?'

Ross was about to answer, but Macleod was looking over his shoulder and could see someone approaching who looked like they were an authority. The woman was tall, almost imperious, and her eyes fixed on Macleod. An officer went to stop her passing through a cordon, but Macleod shouted over and told him to let her through.

'Ah,' said Ross, 'that's Mrs Fotheringham-Smythe. She's the deputy headmistress.'

'I see,' said Macleod. 'Quite formidable by the looks of it.'

'You wouldn't believe how much,' said Ross.

'You,' said the woman. Macleod thought her to be in her sixties, or thereabouts, and her hair was tied back into a bun. She looked very much like an old-school teacher, the sort the movies would have you believe ran the world of education. Macleod didn't think that was modern teaching these days. But then again, he was hardly modern policing, was he? And he was in charge.

'Are you referring to me?' asked Macleod.

'Yes, you. You're obviously important. You've come in that police car. Your man here—'

'Are you referring to Detective Sergeant Ross?' asked Macleod.

'Yes. Well, I've tried to tell him. We have to keep this quiet. We can't let this get out. It won't do the parents of the young women any good. They'll be worried sick. We need to contain it. We need to make sure the press aren't plastering it all over their scandalous pages.'

'I think you'll find that my primary task here is to find out what happened and if any foul play has taken place.'

'Well, I think foul play has taken place. I think that's obvious, isn't it?'

Macleod reached inside his jacket and pulled out his credentials. 'My name's Detective Chief Inspector Seoras Macleod.'

'You're him, aren't you?' said the woman suddenly.

'That's what the credentials say. It's got my photograph,' said Macleod. He didn't know why he was so full of banter. When he came through the gate, he was a little unsettled.

'You're off the telly. You're the one always on the telly. They're always coming to talk to you. Well, I don't need a showman. I need someone to keep this quiet and get this school back on track.'

Showman, thought Macleod. *Is that what I am? A showman? Just because I've done police updates with the press? Briefings on the telly?*

'The school will have to wait and you'll have to cope,' said Macleod. 'First and foremost, I need to see the body and talk with my sergeant about what we're doing here. We will then need to speak to the likes of yourself and others. Ross, make sure you get me that list.'

'Of course, sir,' said Ross.

'And if you don't mind, Mrs Fotheringham-Smythe—is that what you said, Ross?'

'That's it exactly, sir.'

'If you don't mind, ma'am, I'll come to speak to you when I'm ready. But I have to get on with my job. Thank you.'

Macleod turned and walked away. He hated those who thought they were in charge. He was, and couldn't abide other people sticking their oar in. That being said, the woman was looking after the school, so he couldn't fault her.

Macleod entered what he thought to be administrative buildings, given that a larger section of the building was located a short distance away. These looked like small offices, and he was soon pointed through to the office of the headmistress. The door was open, and so he peered inside. He saw Jona Nakamura, Inverness station's forensic lead, and several of her colleagues working in the office. He went to step inside.

'You know the drill,' said Jona without even looking at him. 'Get a coverall on and I'll take you through. Don't come in yet. Not ready for that.'

Macleod was going to say something, but Jona was Jona. She was right.

'I'll just get the coverall, then,' said Macleod. 'Take it you didn't have time to get my coffee on.'

Jona's head spun over, looking directly at him. She gave a grin. 'Coverall,' she said, and then turned back to her work.

Five minutes later, and with his side now hurting a little—he thought he pulled something trying to get into the coverall—Macleod made his way back into the headmistress's office. As he did so, Jona told him to stand in the corner, and Macleod thought he was back at school. Jona, however, didn't keep him waiting and came over, still maintaining her own hood.

Macleod realised that there was a large sheet currently across the room. It looked like a standard office. On the side were shelves with books. There was a smaller table where he thought someone could be entertained, similar to his own office. And there were charts here and there. He recognised admin, for he had to deal with so much of it these days. However, there must have been a main desk, and it was behind the large sheet that was across the room.

'Why is that there?'

'You'll see in a minute,' said Jona. 'We've got the door open, we're working, and I don't want anyone coming past to see it.'

'That bad,' said Macleod.

'No, not that bad. You'll understand when you see it,' said Jona. 'This way.'

She turned and Macleod followed, but he paused when he saw the whiteboard at the side of the office.

'"Slut." I take it there's a sexual motive involved then,' said Macleod. Jona turned back to him.

'You won't believe this,' she said, and then continued around to the other side of the sheet. Macleod stared at the words on the whiteboard for a moment before following her. As he passed the sheet, he stopped suddenly, his mouth agape.

There was a woman straddling a mannequin. She was fully naked, and she was in a sexual position, something you might see in an erotic movie. Her hands were behind her head, but the mannequin had a full view of her body as she straddled it. For a moment, Macleod struggled to process the image. The position she was in was one she would have had to support herself in. And yet, she'd passed.

'You're wondering how she is in that position and how she died?' asked Jona.

'It's one of several things I'm wondering,' said Macleod.

'Her clothes, apparently, were found in the gymnasium.'

'We'll deal with her clothes later. How?' asked Macleod, indicating the body.

'How is she in that position? If you look,' said Jona, 'at the way she's straddled, the legs are actually slightly further forward than they normally would be. She's not raised completely up on her knees. Instead, the legs have formed a solid base.'

Macleod shook his head. 'I'm sorry?'

'She didn't die in the middle of doing something,' said Jona. 'She was not involved in any activity.'

'Then how?'

'If you approach the body, look at the wrists and at the neck. There are places where, clearly, the body's been held with ropes.'

'Let me get this straight. You're telling me that somebody placed a mannequin on the table like this, got her into this position, and held her with ropes.'

'Yes, that's what I believe happened. I need to get the body back to the lab to confirm, but I also believe that she was then poisoned in position.'

'She was poisoned while being held in that position,' said Macleod.

'Yes, the complete system shut down. And then she died just like that. The ropes were then removed. If you set her up right,' said Jona, 'the body can support itself temporarily until the rigor mortis breaks back down. With rigor mortis, everything's locked. That's why her arms are behind her head like that. I can't move them. But they won't stay like that for more than another twelve hours, maybe.'

'You're telling me,' said Macleod, 'that this woman was stripped, placed on top of the mannequin against her will, held with ropes, and then killed by being poisoned.'

'I believe by injection. I think I've found the site. In fact, I think I've got two injection sites. First, you use something to subdue her. If you imagine trying to get someone into a position like that.'

Macleod went to sit down.

'Don't,' said Jona.

'Sorry,' said Macleod. 'Just run this by me again.'

'They would have injected her at some point. A relaxant, something that means she can't move. Something that's going to numb her, going to stabilise her. She's going to be immobile but not dead. They strip her. They've then taken her and placed her in this position. The joints will still be flexible but she can't use them. And then, once they've got her in position, she's tied with ropes. Next, they inject her with poison so that she dies, and then rigor mortis sets in. You can take away the ropes because they've positioned the legs and the centre of gravity of the body so that she won't tumble forward or back. That's not a natural sexual position,' said Jona.

'You have to forgive me,' said Macleod. 'It's been a long time since that was any type of position for me.'

'You would be more upright. The knees would be slightly further back. The knees have been shoved forward to create a stable platform.'

'I get it,' said Macleod. 'As weird as it seems, somebody set up this tableau. Clearly, there's some sort of sexual aspect with the word "slut" over there, and this could be a possible revenge from a lover or someone else.'

'Well, that's your job,' said Jona. 'I wouldn't speculate.'

'Bit young for a headmistress, isn't she?' said Macleod.

'Private school. Private schools can do what they want to a large degree, but she's a good-looking woman. Or she was,' said Jona.

Macleod didn't like to say so, for the woman was dead. But yes, she was very attractive, or she would have been with life in her. She had long, flowing, dirty blonde hair, a trim figure, and was quite buxom. She did not fit his idea of a normal-looking headmistress. But then again, he had seen plenty of different detectives in his time.

Ross was at the door of the office, and Macleod thanked Jona and walked over to him.

'You've seen it then, sir.'

'Yes, Ross, I have. What do you make of it?'

'Looks like somebody was playing around or didn't give back enough affection that somebody was looking for. She was called Georgie Mackie, an orphan, with no family, just herself, and she's been headmistress here for two years. Very well liked from the brief conversations I've had. But then, they always say that after someone's died.'

'I don't like this, Ross,' said Macleod. 'Why? I'm also not sure that one person could have done that. We need to have a proper talk with Jona. We need to find out exactly what happened here, how she was killed, and what was used. I know Jona's got her ideas about her being incapacitated, positioned and then killed, but one person doing that, I'm not sure.'

'Well, I've started to line people up. There's a senior staff here, probably best to talk to them first.'

'Very good, Ross, lead on,' said Macleod.

As Ross led him along corridors with hundreds of school photos up, Macleod could see that Applecross Academy had been there for a while. He also saw that it was a school entirely for girls. *Why did Hope have to be off now?* he thought. *If ever I needed a woman's touch on a case, this is it.*

Chapter 03

Ross opened the door to the staff common room, where he had gathered the senior staff of the school. Macleod followed in and saw faces staring back at him, one of whom he recognised straight away. Julia Fotheringham-Smythe almost glared at him as Macleod entered the room.

'I thank you all for gathering here,' said Ross. 'This is Detective Chief Inspector Macleod, who will run the investigation into the death of your headmistress. The inspector would like to ask you some questions. Perhaps it's best if we introduce exactly who we are to the inspector.'

'I shall introduce the inspector to the staff. After all, my duty as deputy headmistress,' said Mrs Fotheringham-Smythe. 'First, we have Lily Waters, our science head.'

A middle-aged woman of about forty looked over at Macleod. Her short, dark brown hair and trim figure gave her an almost boffin look. She had a thin smile, but her eyes were staring with interest. Macleod almost thought he was being enticed.

'Miss Waters is a former forensic officer, and quite a catch for us to have within the school. A real, proper scientist, as opposed to those who simply get their qualifications.'

Lily smiled again at Macleod. 'Ah, former forensic officer. Which force?' asked Macleod.

'Staffordshire,' said Lily. 'A few years ago, now. I've been a teacher for at least ten years.'

'Well, thank you.'

'Moving on,' said Mrs Fortheringham-Smythe. 'Our head of Mathematics here is Mia Xien—hails from Glasgow, inspector.'

'Spent most of my time in the force in Glasgow,' said Macleod. Mia was an Asian woman, and she looked at Macleod from a rather diminutive stance. That being said, she looked to be strong, muscular, with medium-length black hair that flowed down the back of her neck. A picture of health, but more than that, had an underlying depth to her, a strength inside. Maybe he was just reading too much into her physique.

'What part of Glasgow did you come from?' asked Macleod.

'Lived on the west side for a while, round about before that,' said Mia. 'Ken?'

'I'm sure you can talk more to the inspector when he has time to talk to you, Mia. If I may, Inspector, this is Mr Kershaw, James Kershaw. He's our PE instructor.'

'Well, delighted to meet you, Inspector.'

Macleod shook hands with the man, who could have been half Macleod's age at least, if not more so. He was taller, strong as any PE instructor should be with very short-cut hair.

'We're all deeply saddened to hear of the passing of our headmistress. Special woman,' said James.

'Indeed,' said Macleod, and turned back to Mrs Fotheringham-Smythe.

'And this is our English head, Iris Adams.'

Macleod looked at long red hair tied up in a ponytail that

reminded him of Hope. Like Hope, the woman had a trim figure, but there was almost a shyness to her. Maybe that came from the round glasses she wore, for she seemed to hide behind them. She couldn't have been much older than Kershaw, the PE instructor.

'And this is our Religious Education head, Miss Drummond. She covers other minor subjects as well. That, Inspector, is the senior staff.'

Pauline Drummond stepped forward to Macleod, shaking his hand. Unlike the others, she dressed rather demurely and was a much larger woman. In saying that, Macleod thought she still looked to be in good shape. A brunette with straight hair that was tied up at the back. Not quite in a bun, but a sort of half-ponytail.

'Well, thank you all for assembling,' said Macleod. 'I'd like to talk to you individually. Obviously, at this time, there'll be lots of rumours about. You no doubt will have heard the position your headmistress was found in. That being said, we will proceed with the investigation with no bias. Please be candid when you speak to me.'

'Well, Lily here would be a good person to start with. Or would you rather start with me?' said Mrs Fotheringham-Smythe.

'Well, why not?' said Macleod.

'Obviously, this is a tragedy for the school. A travesty. This sort of occurrence could have a deep impact on the young women. I'm not sure how they'll take it. I mean, it's one thing to be found dead. It's quite something else to be found in that position.'

'Were you aware of any men in the headmistress's life?' asked Macleod.

21

'We didn't talk about her personal life. We talked about the school. School is the life here. There's not much else outside. We lock the gates at night. We open them again in the morning. The young women are here. We live here. And then we have summer recess. Some of us go our separate ways for a couple of months' holiday, see family, and then we come back. School is what it is all about.

'This is a school for excellence, Inspector. Gifted young women. We're taking them in the prime of life when they've just become young women. We nurture them, helping them to go out into the world and be part of it, to succeed in it and to better it. There's no sexual activity on the grounds; hence, there's no need to discuss it, no need to talk about it. We keep our private lives to ourselves as teachers. And while we are here, there is no private life going on. You dedicate yourself to the school.'

'Okay,' said Macleod, feeling he'd just heard a speech.

'So, you're unaware of anything in her personal life. She was an orphan and had no family, I believe.'

'Which is why Miss Mackie was perfect for here,' continued the deputy headmistress. 'She could dedicate herself to the school. The assertion that she was somehow running around with someone is scandalous, and it must not get out. I will not tell the young women the manner of her death. And you shall not tell the papers.'

'Let's get one thing straight,' said Macleod. 'I appreciate you wish to protect the school. However, I will do what I will do in the line of my investigation, and finding the murderer is my key aim. I will shelter your school as best I can, but if those two aims collide, the investigation comes first. Now,' he said before she could reply, 'Miss Waters, shall I speak to you?'

Macleod stepped over to the corner of the room, followed by Lily Waters.

'Well, Inspector, much better to be over here in the corner together. I'm afraid our deputy head does like to be rather grandiose. Have an audience, trying to put you in your place, but I see a man like you has been through that before. You handled it rather superbly.'

'Thank you for the compliment,' said Macleod. 'Can I ask, though, Miss Mackie, what did you make of her?'

'Georgie was quite something. Very pleasant woman. Good to work with. Open to ideas, open to making the place better. I liked the woman. I really did. Played sport with her.'

'Really,' said Macleod. 'What sport did you play?'

'Well, we had occasional bits of tennis and that here in the grounds, but that wasn't serious. Really, we were into judo.'

'Right,' said Macleod. 'You have judo here?'

'James there teaches judo,' said Lily, pointing over to the PE instructor. 'Myself, Mia, Iris, and Georgie were coached out of hours by James. It was good in the evening. There are not many places to go here. You can go into Applecross, but let's be honest, it's not like going to the big city, is it? We tend to, when we're here, stay here. Only go into town for the bare essentials. Send someone else if we have to.'

'And how were your judo sessions?'

'Oh, very amicable. I mean, we all enjoyed it, throwing each other about a bit. I think Mrs Fotheringham-Smythe, however, doesn't appreciate them. Well, she's not of an age to take part, is she? But it was good for Georgie. Us younger women, we need to have a bit of a laugh. You have to be a bit detached from the girls, obviously. And Mrs Fotheringham-Smythe expects you to be like that. It's had a bit of a history, this school. Keep up standards. We'd like to bring things into the modern age, but you have to do it slowly. Georgie was doing it slowly.'

'You've heard how she was found, though,' said Macleod.

'Yes, I heard she was naked on top of a mannequin.'

'There was also the word "slut" written on her whiteboard, which is why I'm asking if you knew anything about Georgie's sexual activity.'

'Georgie was a bit of a flirt, I'll grant you that,' said Lily. 'And a good-looking woman. I take it you've seen her.'

'I saw her body, yes,' said Macleod.

'Well, she was good-looking, but she was no slut. Flirt, yes. She used to flirt with James a lot at the judo. But we all did. Just us winding down. There was nothing in it.'

'But was she having any sexual relationships that you knew of?' asked Macleod.

'No. Not that I knew of. But she was brilliant. She wasn't a prude, you know. The deputy head's a prude—doesn't talk about things like that. That's why she's up in arms at how this affects the school. Could get a bad reputation from this. Well, in truth, the girls liked her because she was a woman. She could be a real woman. Didn't have to be this old-fashioned image. She was good for the girls because she wasn't a prude. No, she wasn't a slut either. Georgie was a confident woman who knew her own sexuality. Just what modern women need to be.'

'May I interrupt?' said a voice.

'No, you may not,' said Lily. Macleod looked over his shoulder and saw Pauline Drummond.

'I feel I have to correct something that Miss Waters is saying,' said Pauline. 'Georgie had taken things too far. Georgie, when she left the school, well, she was always in the latest clothing.

Necklaces, rings, always changing.'

'She liked a bit of bling. It's not a crime,' said Lily.

'It was signalling things.'

'You're just a prude, Pauline. Causing trouble where it's not wanted.'

'Sex is in a rightful place when at home in the marriage. However, because of Georgie, the moral teaching of the girls has suffered.'

'Georgie taught them how to be a modern woman,' said Lily.

'And? What about Keira Saunders then?' said Pauline. 'The poor girl's having a child because of the lack of a moral example.'

'You can't blame Georgie for Kiera getting pregnant.'

'I don't blame her, but she was a bad influence. She was encouraging the girls to show themselves off. You've seen it nowadays. Inspector, the type of clothes that are modern. Well, what man wouldn't enjoy them?'

'Well, I . . .' started Macleod, not quite sure what to say back to that.

'It has nothing to do with that. It's the boys from the nearby electricians. That's all it is, Inspector. The girls pop into the town. There's not much to do. The boys from the electricians, that's the business in town, see the girls go. They're all that age. Late teens, early twenties, of course they mix. And Keira was daft enough not to look after herself.'

'Look after herself?' said Macleod.

'Make sure to use protection. There was nothing unamicable in what they were doing. The boy that she got pregnant with was a decent enough guy.'

'Wild and sowing as oats as ever,' said Pauline.

'Shut up,' said Lily. 'The boy came to see her.'

'He didn't marry her though, did he?'

'Get with the times,' said Lily.

'If he was going to stand by her, he should stand by her properly,' said Pauline.

'I don't think that needs to be up for discussion,' said Mrs Fotheringham-Smythe from the corner.

'It's the inspector,' said Lily. 'He needs to know what's going on. He needs to know what happens. It's not for the press. It was to be expected, boys and girls mingling, sometimes things happen.'

'It doesn't have to happen like that. If we have standards, if we teach them right, things don't go too far too quickly.'

'Get with it, Pauline. That's not life these days. Life these days is to be enjoyed. Georgie taught the girls how to be real women at a proper age, not some backed-up impression of a 1940s woman. We have the vote now, you know that.'

'I tell you this,' said Pauline. 'The only difference between Georgie and you is that Georgie was a young tart, and you, Lily, are an old one.'

Lily jumped forward, fist raised to take a swing at Pauline. Almost imperceptibly, Mia had moved across the room and was now grabbing Lily's arm. Lily struggled to free it, but Mia held it tight.

'Don't,' she said. 'Don't.'

'Indeed,' said Macleod. 'Don't. That's enough from the two of you ladies, I think we'll talk to people on their own if you can't take heated conversations. I'm all for differences of opinion, and emotions will run high at the moment, but let's keep it civil.'

'Shall I procure a room, Inspector?' asked Ross.

'I think so, and maybe somebody to supervise this room

while I'm out of it.'

'That won't be necessary, Inspector,' said Mrs Fotheringham-Smythe. 'I shall ensure there's good behaviour here. Ladies, we have young women to instruct, young women who are waking up to the bad news. Let us be less focused on ourselves.'

Macleod looked at Pauline, and her face was still angry. She was still spitting daggers. Lily, on the other hand, had turned away from her, almost tutting to the air.

Chapter 04

'Do you miss Glasgow?' asked Macleod as Mia Xien entered the room. Macleod held his palm open to show that Mia could sit in a chair on one side of the table while Macleod was on the other. There was a pot of black coffee, and he poured a cup for Mia and one for himself.

'Sometimes,' said Mia, 'especially in moments like today. I'm sorry you had to witness them fighting like that. Not very professional.'

'No. It wasn't really, was it? But let's talk more about you. What did you do before coming here?' asked Macleod.

'I was teaching in Glasgow, several secondary schools, some rough ones, Drumchapel way. Learned to handle people a lot better.'

'That's different from here. Why did you come here?' asked Macleod.

'Quieter life. The girls here are much easier to handle; you can do more with them. A lot of them are, well, very talented. Mathematics can be taken to a higher level. I have a degree in it, so secondary school teaching is fine, but I really like to do more with it. And some of our pupils are very talented. Of course, you get some who aren't so. Mum and Dad paid them in. But for some of them, they really are quite something.'

'So, you came for a quieter life,' said Macleod. 'Have you found it to be that?'

'Generally, yes.'

'Do you like a quiet life, or do you need activity? I heard you enjoy judo.'

'I do,' said Mia. 'And I did judo with Lily, Georgie and Iris. It wasn't my thing at the start, but they were doing it and I had nothing else to do. It got us into a situation where we weren't working with each other. And it was fun. James made it fun. I mean, he's a good-looking bloke, James, and he's good fun when we're doing the judo. We have a laugh.'

'Only the four of you do it, though. What about the others on the staff? Junior teachers, or others from the senior staff as well. No one else want to?'

'What James really wanted was just a small group. He didn't want to teach a big class. He did it initially as a favour and then we all seemed to get on. Obviously, Mrs Fotheringham-Smythe, the deputy head, will not want to do it. And, well, Pauline. Pauline wouldn't.'

'She wouldn't?'

'No,' said Mia. 'Sport's not her thing. I mean, a bigger woman who doesn't run around a lot.'

'I wouldn't have said she was unfit,' said Macleod. 'Seemed in reasonable shape.'

'Not really into the idea of a man teaching women to throw each other around. Which, is surprising though as she likes James.'

'Does everyone like James?'

'Well, Inspector, he's a good-looking man. But, I mean, Pauline was jealous. She didn't like the time we spent with him, and yet it wasn't something she was going to do. I think she'd like to be manhandled by him, if you ask me. But on her own.'

'Did Georgie?' asked Macleod.

'Georgie had fun with James. But Georgie was the head-mistress, James's boss. Georgie could wind down, could be a different person outside of the school. And when I say outside of the school, the judo really was us no longer being in our roles. It was our minor break at the end of a day. Pauline didn't like that. She didn't like how Georgie was being familiar with James. She said it compromised Georgie. I think she was just annoyed that Georgie got a lot closer to James then her.'

'Forgive me,' said Macleod. 'I wouldn't have thought that Pauline was like that. She seemed to be very anti-extramarital affairs. Is she married?'

'She used to be a vicar's wife, according to rumour,' said Mia. 'I work with her professionally. I don't get heavily involved in talking to her about anything else. But if she was, she's gone back to being a Miss.'

'Clearly, she's made an impression on you.'

'And she made an impression on Georgie. As you've seen from the outburst, she clashes over Georgie's modern outlook. Georgie could dress well, you know. And Georgie wasn't afraid to look good, Inspector. Pauline's right in the sense that, well, nowadays, what women consider being correct and proper to wear differs greatly from the older styles. But they're still correct and proper to them, I guess. That's where the clash happened.'

'Just over clothing. Seems somewhat petty. Seems—'

'Well, there were a few other things,' said Mia.

'Such as,' asked Macleod.

'The accommodation blocks where we all live. The senior staff have got slightly bigger homes because that's what they are. They're our home. We're based here now. The headmistress's has its own bit of garden. And Georgie saw that as her place. She used to like to sunbathe in front of it.'

'And?' said Macleod, wondering if the west coast somehow got a lot better weather than Inverness.

'Well, the trouble is that the front garden is overlooked. When the girls walk about, they can see into it.'

'And. What? She was inappropriate, according to Pauline.' Mia nodded. 'Why, what did she do?' asked Macleod.

'Georgie liked to get a tan, and she would happily lie in the sun when we got it, which isn't that often.'

'So Pauline was annoyed she was wearing a bikini,' said Macleod.

'She was initially, but she was more annoyed,' said Mia, 'when she wasn't wearing a bikini.'

'What?' blurted Macleod. 'She went starkers?'

'No, no, you misunderstand. Georgie used to tan face down, but with her top off, so that her back would get an unbroken tan. She was perfectly decent in that she would put it back on before she got up or, else pop on a t-shirt or something. She wasn't parading around; she was just lying sunbathing. Now, most of the rest of us can get over that, but Pauline thought it was dreadful that the girls could walk past and see her like that.'

'Do you know what the girls thought of it?'

'Most of the girls didn't think much of it. I mean, they've seen a lot worse back at home or whatever. They're not prudes, the girls, they're young girls. You know, Georgie was doing nothing wrong; it's just the likes of Pauline kicked off.'

31

'What did Mrs Fotheringham-Smythe think of it?' asked Macleod.

'Well, I never spoke to her directly about it, but she didn't get up in arms about it. Maybe she thought that was Georgie's space and she could do as she pleased within reason. As I said, I thought Pauline was very out of line. It wasn't like Georgie was doing anything she shouldn't. But then again, Pauline used to be a vicar's wife. Well, where he is now, who knows?'

'But you can think of nothing that Georgie did that would have deemed her to be a slut in someone's eyes.'

'In Pauline's eyes, maybe. But Pauline wouldn't have written that. That's the thing. Pauline wouldn't say that. Say something like Jezebel, harlot, something biblical, maybe.'

Macleod next interviewed Iris Adams, the English head, who sat down opposite his desk, fiddling with her ponytail. She almost hid behind the glasses, but when she stared at him, they made her eyes look large, almost like an owl.

'How are you doing?' asked Macleod. 'Bit of a shock.'

'Yes,' she said. 'A lot of a shock.'

'How well did you know the headmistress?'

'We worked together, we did judo together.'

'With James, the PE instructor?'

'Yes,' said Iris. Macleod thought she looked a little embarrassed.

'What is the judo to you?' asked Macleod.

'A way to stay fit, it's enjoyable.'

'Because you're with friends?' The woman nodded. 'And James is a good instructor?' asked Macleod.

The woman beamed for a moment and then suddenly retracted as if she'd let something out.

'Have you ever been instructed by anyone else?' She shook

her head. 'And he's what?'

'He's rather dishy, isn't he?' said Iris suddenly. 'Shouldn't say it, should we? But he is. And it's nice when he, well, teaches us, throws us about at the judo class.' She looked like she was about to giggle.

'Is there anything more than that between James and you?'

'Oh no. No, no, Inspector,' she said. 'Absolutely not. I keep myself to myself when I'm here. Mrs Fotheringham-Smythe was very blunt when I first arrived. I was here before the headmistress.' Iris suddenly went silent again.

'You've heard about how the headmistress died,' said Macleod. The woman nodded, looking down now at the table, rather than at Macleod. 'She was in quite a position, and the word slut was written on her whiteboard. It's quite a strong word.'

'It is.'

'Would she be doing anything to justify that comment?' asked Macleod.

Iris went suddenly red. She looked over her glasses at Macleod, her hand going to her mouth. 'I shouldn't say.'

'This is a murder investigation, you probably should say,' said Macleod, 'in fact, definitely say.'

'But it's only hearsay; they don't like hearsay in court, do they?'

'We're not in court. I'm running an investigation. I'm trained in how to handle hearsay, so please, say away.'

'Well,' said Iris, 'I don't like to talk ill of the dead, and Georgie was such a nice person, but, well, I saw nothing. Some girls did say . . .'

'Girls said what?'

'Some girls talked about her seeing someone. With the way

she was dressing, at times, that was how she looked.'

'What times?'

'Oh, they never said when. They never. Just general conversation. Little bits overheard. I didn't believe them. I didn't want to believe them. Innocent until proven guilty, isn't it?' said Iris. 'And the girls, they talk. Well, Pauline talks about girls not saying this, not saying that. Girls are like boys. We say stuff, you know, especially at that age. We talk about things, sex being one of them.'

'Would you have considered Georgie to be a flirt?' asked Macleod.

'Yes, she could flirt with men, wasn't completely obvious,' said Iris. 'I'm woeful at it. I just get embarrassed.'

'Why?' asked Macleod. 'I mean, clearly, you're a woman of the world, good-looking. Why would you get embarrassed?'

'I used to be a nun when I was a late teenager. Became a nun, but I left that all five years ago, and I just, well, had enough and hadn't seen the real world. I wanted more. I wanted out. So I ended up teaching here. I was teaching when I was a nun. I came out, I needed a job, and I got recruited to Applecross by Georgie. So it's hard to say things about her.'

'What was she like then, when she interviewed you? Why did she want you here?'

'Funny enough, she said I'd be good for them. I had a good moral code. My being a nun, but I wasn't ridiculous. She said I could be modern with them. I could be honest with them. I guess maybe she wanted a slight difference to herself. Her being a very modern woman, and me being the one considering whether you should be modern. It's a shame, though. She was very good with them. I liked her a lot.'

'Pauline Drummond seems to have a very religious side to

her. Certainly a strong moral code, whether it be right or not,' said Macleod. 'You see eye to eye with her?'

'I left because of people like Pauline. You're a nun, it's important to reach out, not to condemn. And yet, there's so much condemnation going on. I can mix freely now with people. I understand her, Pauline but I just think she's wrong. She's wrong about Georgie.'

'Do you know that for sure, though?' asked Macleod. 'Do you know Georgie wasn't having relations with anyone?'

'I don't think she was. I don't see how we have the time for it. I certainly didn't. And I certainly don't have the time.'

'Can I make an observation?' asked Macleod.

'It's your interview, Inspector.'

'Would it be correct in saying that James was like a, well, a night out for you ladies? You don't seem to have much entertainment here. So going to the judo with a nice-looking young man was a bit of entertainment.'

Iris beamed. Her cheeks were burning red. 'It was for me, Inspector. It was for me.'

'And for Georgie?'

'Oh, she enjoyed it, whether or not she had anything going on beyond it, I don't know, but I doubt it; she was busy too; she loved the job; she wouldn't have risked it for that.'

Macleod didn't believe that. People risk things all the time. Stupid risks, daft risks. He'd have to find out if Georgie was risking anything, had she stepped too far, or was this something else entirely?

Chapter 05

Susan Cunningham gave a yawn while she was hunched over and turned away from those around her. She had set off from Inverness that morning with Perry, and on arrival, they'd been working hard at the scene of the crime. Everyone had been waiting for Macleod to arrive, but nonetheless, Susan and Perry had been kept busy, with Ross giving them jobs to do. Susan was now to go through the girls at the school and interview them in large groups.

It wasn't a task she looked forward to. Susan could remember being that age, could remember all the rumours, the gossip, the talk, remembered how a lot of it just wasn't true. A lot of it was fanciful. There were some girls who were desperately interested in boys. Some girls desperately interested in girls. And other girls just not interested in that at all, thinking about other things.

There was the make-up, the fashion. There had been so much running through her head. How you looked, what you said, what you did. Susan was very glad the teenage years were behind her. However, she didn't blame them. For many years, Susan had been the one who had to look a certain way, had to appear a certain way to the boys. She'd sought to find relationships there but ended up just in one torrid relationship after another. And when she looked back on it, being used by the worst sort of man.

Coming back reminded her of a time she didn't need to remember. She'd moved on. She'd lost a leg in the line of duty, and yet here she was with her prosthetic, working away. Susan was what they would have called a good news story. A credit to the force. Not what she thought she used to be. But it always lingered there in the background. The past was never something that truly disappeared. It always came after you. Even if it was several hundred innocent schoolgirls that were helping it to return.

Susan spent half an hour talking to some sixteen-year-old girls, the youngest age and the lowest year group. The years were split into three, with about a hundred in each, which was too many for Susan to talk to at once. So instead, she had split those years up, so she only had about fifteen at a time.

The second batch had been a lively sort. Some girls had got a scholarship to school and came from poorer homes. Most seemed to have been out of the Glasgow area, some from Edinburgh, some from slightly further afield, and only a few from around Applecross itself. A lot of the girls, though, had rich parents, and she could tell the difference.

They talked as if money was no object. She also thought that they weren't that sharp, some of them. Although in fairness what did she know? She was only interviewing them about a murder. Most of the girls seemed to like their deceased headmistress. There were tears, moments when the girls hugged each other.

'She was fantastic to us, really good. Let us do exciting stuff, and she looked cool. She dressed cool. She was just one of those people,' said one girl. Another commented 'how we could go to the large festivals. Got down to Glasgow and Edinburgh, sometimes up to Inverness. Yes, occasionally even further afield. It was tremendous. But that Smythe wouldn't let us do that. No, no, that's only since Miss Mackie came in.'

The older year groups were the same. They said that since Miss Mackie had come, they'd got to do a lot more. Although in the past, elders had let them choose certain travels. But things had increased. The school was flourishing. There was also chatter about Mr Kershaw, which Susan put down to the usual girly gossip. There weren't that many men around the building. And Donnie, well, she'd seen the caretaker that morning. And while he might have been a very pleasant person, while he may have been a good companion, he wasn't what a teenage girl was looking for. On the other hand, James Kershaw looked like a stud. *That's what they called those men back then, wasn't it?* thought Susan. She wasn't that far away from this.

And Susan got to speak to the older ones, those in their final year. They were a bit more sombre when they talked about the headmistress. They all loved her. All loved how she dressed. They all loved that, in the summer, when the heatwave had arrived, she wasn't bothered about them all lying around sunbathing. Old Battleaxe Smythe had gone through the roof. Some girls made mention of how she'd been found. Susan tried not to say too much, for strictly the scene of the death hadn't been officially told to anyone, but rumour had got out.

'I don't remember her having a mannequin in there. She could have pulled a real man. She didn't need a false one,' said one girl.

'Jen, it's not a blow-up doll. It was just a prop they put in there; they were trying to say something.'

'She was no slut, tell you that. Miss was not that. She was

classy. She was the best.'

Susan could see others weren't speaking, holding their tongue. Some because it looked like they were about to burst into tears, but others had that look of disagreement, but the quiet kind you exercise when in a large group.

When the last of the oldest ones had been through, Susan made her way to the toilets and found a cubicle to sit down in. As she sat there, she heard somebody walk into the toilets. The cubicle door beside hers opened, and then someone sat down. Susan thought nothing of it until she heard a voice.

'Are you the detective? Is that you in there?' said a girl's voice quietly.

'Yes, I'm the detective. Detective Constable Susan Cunningham.'

'You were talking to us. I need to speak to you.'

'Well, maybe we could speak outside,' said Susan.

'Not where people can see us. Can't do that. I need you to speak here.'

'No,' said Susan, 'anyone could walk in and I'm in the middle of something, so I'll be outside, walk past me and tell me somewhere quiet to go and I'll follow you.'

'Okay.'

'What's your name?' said Susan quickly.

'Kim.'

Susan hurried through what she had to do and after washing her hands, stepped outside the toilets. Almost immediately somebody walked past her and said to her, 'the bushes through the second door.' Susan watched the girl walk along. She was one of the older ones and the girl glanced back over her shoulder once to see if Susan was following. She then took a right through the doors and by the time Susan had got there, she saw her disappear behind a set of bushes outside. Susan was beside her thirty seconds later.

'You've got me then,' said Susan. 'What is it you need to tell me?'

'When she was found, they said she was found with the word slut on the whiteboard. Is that right?'

'I can't say that. I can't say it was or it wasn't,' said Susan. 'That's confidential information to the case.'

'Well, everybody knows it. It's what they're all saying. Saying she was naked too. Naked on top of a mannequin like they were doing it.'

'What is it you want to tell me?' said Susan. 'Or have you just got me here to try to get information out of me?'

'You need to investigate further. You need to look at Mr Kershaw.'

'Why?' asked Susan.

'She was…'

'She was what?'

'She was banging him.'

'You're saying that Mr Kershaw and Miss Mackie were lovers?'

'I don't know if it was that,' said Kim. 'She was banging him.'

'How do you know?' asked Susan.

'Everyone knows. She used to go and meet him every night, nearly. In the gymnasium.'

Susan thought about something Macleod had said to her in a mini-briefing earlier on. 'She went to do judo, though.'

'With him,' said Kim.

'Well, she took along a couple others of your teachers. So unless there was something really special going on, it looks like a judo session to me.'

'Maybe they weren't doing it there, but they were doing it. They were definitely doing it. Everybody knows they were doing it. And that Mr Kershaw, oh, Mr Kershaw's in heaven here.'

'In what way?' asked Susan.

'The gym teacher, isn't he? Every time we get changed, he is there, watching us come out. Running around. Likes to see us sweat. But you see him; he's watching everyone. All the teachers too. Well, the good-looking ones. The man's never not looking. Teaches us PE and he teaches us swimming. He loves swimming. Absolutely loves the swimming.'

'Has he ever been inappropriate to you? Has he ever touched any of you? Has he ever said anything that was not right?'

Kim shook her head. 'No. But he watches. He's always watching. Talks to you. He doesn't look at your face. Likes to make us run around. He's a dirty pervert. They all say that. He's a dirty pervert.'

'That's strong words to call somebody a pervert if they haven't done anything. I mean, if you look at a man, are you a pervert?'

'It's not what I mean. I don't make people run around and sweat. And besides, he's . . . well, I think he's . . .'

'You think he's what?' asked Susan.

'I think he and some of the girls have, you know.'

'That's not illegal. It's not right from an employment point of view. It is a workplace, but—and don't get me wrong, I'm not saying he's correct to do it—but none of you are underage here. You don't attend until you're sixteen.'

'I'm sure he's been at it with several of them.'

'That's not something you want to go around saying out loud until you've got proof,' said Susan. 'You might be right, but you haven't proved it to me, and I can't go anywhere with that.'

'No, but he's a dirty pervert. He's also a hot one, though,' said Kim.

'I'll bear in mind what you said, but only with the weight it deserves,' said Susan. 'You've given me no evidence.'

The girl disappeared off, and Susan was bemused at what she had said. Is she genuinely worried? Did she fish for information? Was that what was happening? Was she looking to see what reactions she could get out of Susan? Susan had tried to be as professional as possible, but in truth she was tired.

Susan stayed outside the building, taking in a bit of air. It was cool, and she sat and wondered about what she'd heard. All through the day the girls had been emotional. Some had cried, but also they'd talked about how great the headmistress was. There weren't many who had anything negative to say about her. In fact, Susan was struggling to see a dichotomy and what suddenly was this is wild side to her? Was she cheating on someone? How did she have time being a headmistress?

Susan looked at her watch. Macleod would call them all together tonight, and she wondered what she had. Just some wild rumours. Wild rumours set against the fact that most people said how wonderful Georgie Mackie was. Maybe they had more of an opportunity. There'd been a few press too. They'd called by, but so far the circumstances of the death had been kept under wraps. But there was no way it would stay like that, surely. A place like this, this many young girls. People were going to ask, why was Macleod down? Unless it was a suspicious death.

'You all right?' said a voice.

There was Perry.

'Yes,' she said. 'I've finished interviewing all the girls.'

'Find out much?'

'Well-liked generally. Occasionally a wild rumour involving Mr Kershaw. I think a lot of them like Mr Kershaw. But some say he's a pervert.'

'There are three hundred girls here,' said Perry. 'You're going to have how many opinions? Anything to say he is?'

'No,' said Susan. 'Just how he looks at people. One said that her headmistress was having relations with him.'

'It's all strange,' said Perry. 'It's a difficult place if she was messing about with somebody else. Not easy to keep things hidden. Not in a big place like this, with so many people.'

'No,' said Susan. 'Any word from the big boss? When he wants us all together.'

'Ten o'clock. Apparently, I have to get some food for it.'

'Do you know where you're getting it from?' asked Susan.

'Going to drive into Applecross now. You coming?'

'Don't see why not, I'll just square it with Ross.' Susan made a call, before joining Perry in the car.

'You all right?' said Perry. 'You look a little, well, you know, a little shaken; wasn't the body, was it?'

'No, no, we've seen plenty of that stuff.'

'Well, what's up?' asked Perry. 'It's not us, is it? It's not . . .'

'No, Perry, I . . . I've come to terms with that, you know, working here with you now, it's fine; it's fine; it's just that, well, being here reminds me of what I used to be. Some of the girls, it's all gossip and panic and how do I look?'

'But, that's well past you,' said Perry. 'You moved on from that. Look at you now. You're . . .'

'Not quite Tanya,' said Susan suddenly.

'That's not fair,' said Perry. 'That's not fair.'

43

'No, it's not,' said Susan. 'Sorry.'

'Then, what is it?'

'You ever think sometimes the past comes back at you? Have you ever sat with regrets?'

'I try not to,' said Perry. 'You make decisions. Sometimes you get it right. Sometimes you get it wrong.'

'I know,' said Susan. 'It's just seeing what they wrote on that board about her. I was that. I was . . .'

'Lonely,' said Perry. 'You were lonely. And you made bad choices, yes. And you regret that. But you were lonely. Now you need to decide how you will make yourself not lonely. What you'll do. Immerse yourself in your work. Find someone. Do some good.'

Susan put her hand over and touched Perry's. 'That's why I liked you. Do you know that? You build people up, Perry. You're able to get underneath them. You understand people. That's why I fell for you in the end.'

'And there was me thinking it was this unbelievable body,' said Perry. 'Kershaw's got nothing on me.'

Susan punched his arm. It was getting too serious, and he'd broken the mood. That was Perry, always good at avoiding the big conversation, especially if it's one he didn't want to have.

Chapter 06

Macleod entered the classroom that the team had taken over. Ross had set up a base as usual, with some laptops and a mobile whiteboard, sitting in the barren room. This would be a meeting of just the team, and not of the uniformed officers who were helping them.

Ross was still writing on the whiteboard when Macleod entered. He turned briefly, but Macleod waved his hand, indicating that Ross should continue. Macleod made his way over to the small filter coffee machine. It lived now in the back of Ross's car, and then if they were called anywhere, coffee was always available. It made Macleod laugh. There wasn't much you could do for him, but making sure the cup of coffee arrived at the right time could get you well on the way to promotion.

Perry was already there, writing something down. Susan was working on her laptop.

'Jona?' asked Macleod to the air.

'Be here in a couple of minutes,' said Ross, without looking round. 'The coffee's on. Still hot.'

Macleod poured himself a cup and then walked over to a chair near the front. A table hadn't been pulled together. Instead, the classroom was still set out in its rows. Macleod decided to sit on top of one of the desks instead of using the seat.

He sat thoughtfully with his coffee. *Three hundred teenage girls*, he thought, *in this school. That's about 299 more than I can cope with.* He was glad Susan was there, but he deeply regretted Hope being off. *Was there paranoia amongst them? They were at an age that he just didn't work well with. Maybe it was because he'd never been a parent. Maybe he didn't understand them. Well, no, he didn't understand them. That was fair.* The only one with a kid in the room, of course, was Ross. His child was nowhere near that age.

'Sorry I'm late,' said Jona, entering the room. The diminutive Asian woman smiled at Macleod as he turned to look at her. 'I take it the coffee's still good,' she said.

'Have you got the body ready to move?' he said.

'Yes, I might try to race up after her tonight, if you can spare me. I think the rest of the team won't be heading up the road for a bit after that. Maybe in the next day or two.'

'Shall we begin then,' said Macleod, after seeing that nobody else had reacted to Jona's arrival.

'Very good, sir,' said Ross, and he turned to Perry and Susan. 'Shall we bring it a bit closer?'

Perry sighed, stood up, and made his way to sit across from Macleod. Susan joined him, sitting beside him, and Jona arrived with her coffee.

'Shall we start with you, Jona?' said Macleod. 'Where are we at?'

'I'm fairly confident that our victim was immobilised with drugs, placed in the position on top of the mannequin, and held in position by some ropes. Whether the ropes were tied to the room, I'm not sure. I can't find evidence of that. They could have been held by others. Or there could have been another frame, or something brought in that's then taken away.'

'So, we still think that. We still think that the victim is placed up there alive?' asked Macleod.

'Oh yes,' said Jona. 'Definite. Then killed in position. Killed in position, so she's then frozen like a tableau.'

'What does that say then?' asked Perry.

'Say,' said Ross. 'Clearly they didn't like them, and they wanted to make a point.'

'No, seriously,' said Perry. 'You make a point. If you were wanting to say that somebody was a slut as they put it, then have them lying there with nothing on. Have them, I don't know, surrounded by naughty magazines, stuff like that. But to actually bring a mannequin in and set it up. What is this actually saying?'

'It's trying to make the point, isn't it?' said Susan. 'It's making the point. It's displaying them as they really are. In the eyes of the person who's doing the killing.'

'In the eyes of the person, or people?' asked Macleod. 'Jona, could you effectively have created that tableau as a single person?'

'Yes,' said Jona. 'Not easy, but yes. I mean, if you're dedicated enough to knock somebody out and mobilise them and then do this. Well, yeah. It has to be well planned. So, you'd have to be quick. You're operating in the dark. They're doing it in an office. The office is closed down at night. I was told that the whole place is locked up last thing at night. The whole place is then opened in the morning. You've got a window. Nobody's going to be in that office overnight.'

'The campus here at Applecross Academy,' said Macleod, 'has different areas. You've got where the girls' dorms are. There's where the staff live. You've got the school itself, and you've got the admin block.'

'The school's used a bit at night because you've got the gymnasium over there. The admin block isn't,' said Ross.

'That's important, isn't it? That's important because . . .?' asked Macleod.

'It's important,' said Perry, 'because you don't have time to set this up. You would have to do it quickly in the gymnasium . But you could have done this, set it all up, and then thrown the clothes into the gymnasium. That wouldn't take any time at all.'

'You'd have to have keys to the building,' said Susan.

'As I understand it. It's not a very modern place,' said Perry. 'A lot of them are old door keys. Easy to work your way around to finding those, copying them.'

'Check the locksmiths in the local area and beyond, Ross. If you're going to copy them, you'd have to do it quickly.'

'Or cut them yourself,' said Susan, 'if you've got that skill.'

'Place is also clean,' said Jona. 'I need to check for poisons, but I have got the two injection sites. I'm convinced this is how it happened.'

'So you need to know,' said Macleod, 'the dose you'd have to give the patient. Yes, if you're immobilising them. I mean, I'm sure you need leave some sort of flexibility to put them in that position, don't you?'

'You do,' said Jona. 'You need to maintain the flexibility of the joints, kill them afterwards, and then rigor mortis sets in. But you're holding them in a position until rigor mortis has set in, and then they're like an ornament. They have the knee and the back of the feet bent correctly. Side of the leg, too. You have a centre of gravity then maintained within a kind of triangular base. Means they are not going to topple until the rigor mortis fades.'

'This is awfully complex,' said Perry, 'isn't it? I mean, wouldn't you do something else? Wouldn't you?'

'How else would you say it?' asked Macleod.

'There's plenty of ways to say it. I mean, you said it with the whiteboard,' said Perry. 'A four-letter word said everything. You didn't need to make a tableau.'

'So why make it?' asked Macleod. There was silence in the room for a moment.

'I got a rumour today,' said Susan, 'told by a young girl called Kim. She said, in her words, that Georgie was banging Mr Kershaw. Mr Kershaw is a pervert. Mr Kershaw is this, that, and whatever. It's unsubstantiated. It's a rumour. But she says everybody knows. And none of the girls talk about that. None of them talked about that in front of me.'

'Now with the nature of the death,' continued Susan, 'you would have thought that would have been all the rage. There seems to be a silence on that front. Georgie Mackie seems to have been well-liked. But we need to get a better picture of Georgie in our daily life here. We've heard how she caused upset with tradition when she was sunbathing in her front garden. We heard how she likes to send people away on travel. Opened the school up, and there's a tension. How much did Mrs Frotherington-Smith actually kick back? She's the deputy head. She'd be the one who would do.'

'Could you have kept yourself sexually active in the way that's being showed by her death and still run the school? It doesn't happen at schools. People see things. People always see something, don't they?' said Perry.

'That's what we tell ourselves. That's what's on the TV, isn't

49

it? Because if people don't see something, then you can't solve the case,' said Susan.

'No,' said Perry. 'People do see things. Sometimes they don't say them, but they do see them. And then when you get a death, then they think twice.'

'Well, they need to confess,' said Ross.

'Or the opposite,' said Susan. 'They need to keep their heads down even more.'

'There was also the Keira Saunders issue,' said Macleod. 'The girl got pregnant. It caused some ruckus. There was a fight in the staff room over what seemed like two factions. I'm wondering if that's where it's coming from? Did somebody take great offence? After all, Georgie Mackie is the figurehead of the school. She's the headmistress. If she's not adhering to standards and you're of that ilk, maybe that would drive you to—'

'Kill her,' said Ross. 'Why would you kill her? You'd get her sacked. Just come forward with what evidence you've got and say, look at this, can we get rid?'

'He makes a very convincing point,' said Perry. 'Why kill? If you're going to kill her, there's got to be something else. If the problem is her being there, if you simply got rid of her by providing evidence and showing that she was doing the wrong thing, well, you'd win. And you are seen as a good egg. But when you kill somebody, nobody's going to see you as a good egg. It's an extreme way to get rid of somebody you can't get rid of any other way.'

'Could be vengeance, of course. Could be jealousy,' said Susan. 'Maybe the Kershaw thing's true. There were four of them doing judo with Kershaw.'

'And you think they're all doing it because they like him,' said

Perry. 'Friction, then. Maybe he's got extracurricular activities with them, beyond the judo.'

'No evidence of that,' said Macleod. 'That's just a wild theory at the moment.'

'I wouldn't say wild,' said Perry.

'Fancy, call it what you will,' said Macleod. 'It's got nothing to back it up. We need to dig deeper. Let's go talk to Keira Saunders. Find out how she was treated regarding her pregnancy because that could be key. You can see who is on what side and how much they're on that side.'

'There's another angle to look at as well,' said Jona.

'What's that?' asked Macleod.

'Well, I know I'm not one of the detectives here. I don't want to tell you how to do your job. But Mrs Fotheringham-Smythe managed to get into my ear about traditions being lost, got into my ear about how the school had ways of doing things. Do you love your school enough to be able to take somebody out of the way? Is this just about image? Does there need to be actual physical activity in the background to have caused one to think like this? Or is it just suspected? Is it just a general malaise?'

'I don't know,' said Macleod. 'What I do know is we should also talk to the janitor. Perry, you can do that. You're good with people.'

'So people have alleged,' said Perry.

'The janitor, from what I'm told, is not the brightest. Now, I don't know if that's just slanderous, and he's just a bit slow, or if there's something, a condition he's got. But he opens up every day, I was told, and he closes up at night. He's wandering about here all the time. He has no loyalties to the staff. From a work point of view, he's just a janny at the end of the day. You might get a better view from him.'

'I've got accommodation sorted nearby,' said Ross.

'Where?' asked Macleod.

'There's a couple of guest bedrooms over in the accommo-dation. Yours is round on the staff side. There's a dorm not that far from the girls the rest of us can take. Don't worry, it's got a separate sleeping area for Susan. Only if she needs it.'

'Did you sort that out?' asked Macleod to Ross.

'Yes.'

'You should have got Susan or Perry to do that. It's not a sergeant's job.'

'I sorted it out in no time. I deployed them where I thought they'd be at their best. I thought as a sergeant I was meant to organise.'

'It's okay. At the end of the day, it's up to Hope and you how you run the team. I'm just dropping in.'

Macleod stood up and drank his coffee. 'Is there a reason to expose a scandal here? What are we looking at, people? Are we looking at somebody trying to expose something? Are we looking at somebody trying to get revenge against a cheating lover? Are we looking at someone who has an angst against the school?'

'It could be something else, couldn't it?' said Perry.

'At the moment,' said Macleod. 'Could be anything. A lot more work tomorrow, everyone. Get a good night's sleep.'

Chapter 07

Perry shambled over to what he believed was the janitor's lodging. He had eaten no breakfast. He barely got out of bed, dressed himself and said he'd have a shower later on, as well as something to eat. Feeling dishevelled, at least then he felt how people thought of him. He knew he was Perry, a ragamuffin type of person. He liked being that. It threw them off guard. They didn't see the thinking man underneath. But today the thinking man was going to have to go under the skin of Donnie the janitor.

Perry stood outside the man's front door. The night previous when Perry had contacted him, Donnie had said he would do his rounds and that Perry could walk and talk with him. But he was busy, and he had jobs to do.

Perry waited outside the door until Donnie emerged, a large bunch of keys in his hands.

'Hello, Inspector,' said Donnie.

'Constable,' said Perry. 'I'm just a constable. Thank you for letting me walk round with you.'

Donnie gave a shy nod. 'I'm not doing all of my doors today,' he said. 'They said your people are here. They've guarded some of it. I'm not to open the admin rooms. Those keys are with your people.'

'Good,' said Perry. 'I'll just come with you, and we'll talk.'

They strolled, and Donnie led them down to the front gates. 'Always start with these.'

'I guess on the move you'll have seen things,' Perry said.

'Donnie sees lots of things,' Donnie said. 'People don't look at Donnie. Not really. They don't think of Donnie as looking.'

Perry nodded. That sounded about right.

'What can you tell me about the place, then? Was it a big shock when your headmistress was murdered?'

'I still don't understand,' said Donnie, fumbling for his keys. He inserted one in the lock of the front gate, and Perry heard it clunk.

'Why like that? Why? And that word. I asked what that word meant. They told me.'

'Was she like that?' asked Perry.

'No. But this, this was coming.'

'What do you mean, Donnie? What do you mean it was coming?'

'The school was—has been—always very staid, very the same. The headmistress was different, caused trouble amongst people, but not just her. Mr Kershaw is different too, male PE teacher, why,' said Donnie. 'Girls' school.'

'You have a male janitor,' said Perry.

'I don't teach,' said Donnie, 'I just open gates, I just protect the place.'

'But you said that you weren't surprised. What was the headmistress like?'

He stopped only for a moment. It was clear to Perry that he was thinking.

'Miss Mackie was a good-looking woman. Very. But she

had eyes that sought everywhere. That's what my mother said. Eyes that weren't happy to look in their own box. Wanted to look in everyone's boxes. Wanted you to come and look in her box.'

'You mean she was flirting?'

Donnie looked at Perry for a moment. 'She wanted to see who was available, who was happy.'

'Okay, but she was also a woman who did what she wanted. Do you mean she wasn't someone who offered herself up, but she tempted and then she did what she wanted?'

'But she was nice to me,' said Donnie. 'When she first came. I was and still am, on the outside of the staff. I don't get to be in the staff room. I have my place. I have a janitor's place. If she would come to the janitor's place, she would say hello. The others didn't take to her at first. She also could talk to me about the weather. I don't get involved in the school affairs. I don't get involved with the girls. Never, never,' said Donnie.

'Some of them are quite pretty,' said Perry.

Donnie shook his head. 'Trouble. All trouble. Just trouble. You need a woman of your age. Mum always said that.'

'How do the staff treat you, then?'

'They think I'm slow,' said Donnie. 'I am not slow in that sense. I'm not stupid. Difficulty talking, especially in company where I have great difficulty. So Miss Mackie never had me talk to her at a meeting. She would talk to me on my own, during the walk, like you do now. We would meet in the morning.'

'You would arrange a meeting,' said Perry.

'No, we would just meet. She knew what I did. I walk the same route every day, except today because of your police officers.'

'Sorry about that,' said Perry. 'When she met you, what did

she talk about?'

'Anything not to do with the school. I think I was like an outside friend.'

'If she met you on the walk, does that mean sometimes she was in her office early?'

'She had never gone to the office before meeting me. Always would meet me. I think she thought I would be thrown completely. I think she thought I would struggle not meeting her first. She would be somewhere she shouldn't be. I'm not good socially, but I can deal with change,' said Donnie.

'In the staff room yesterday, my boss had a confrontation. There was a row between Miss Drummond and Miss Waters.'

'Miss Drummond, she doesn't like the rest. She's religious. She says too much. Miss Drummond said a lot against the headmistress, too.

'She wasn't happy about the way she sunbathed or the way she behaved when in her own place, not just within the school,' said Perry.

'She had behaved inappropriately,' said Donnie. 'In the school never would somebody behave like that, but she was modern. But she did not. She was no slut, as that word said. They said it meant sleeping around. They said it meant many different men. She would not. She knew what she wanted.'

'Did you say anything else when she came here? When she talked to you?'

'She said to me she was surprised to get the job. It was way above her level. But she told me there was a tax for everything. I don't know what she meant by that.'

Donnie stopped suddenly and pointed to some larger build-ings. 'Those are the dorms. That's where the girls are. I don't open them up. They open them up themselves from inside.'

'Fair enough,' said Perry. 'You don't want to walk in on one of them unsuspectingly.'

'No,' said Donnie. 'But look,' he said. 'I think there are ways from there out past the wall.'

'Why do you say that?'

'The girls. Some of the girls, they meet the boys from the electricians. The boys from the electricians, they see the girls. They think, oh, you know, but they meet up separate. That's what happened. They knew they had met because one had a baby. Well, is having a baby.'

'You think they go over there often?' asked Perry.

'I don't know. Some nights.'

'Do you think any boys come into the dorms?'

'I don't know,' said Donnie. 'I've not found out how they do it. But I swear people come and go, but not the normal way. There is something different.'

'Anything else you don't understand?' asked Perry.

'When they come here, they get a bag.'

'Well, that's pretty normal,' said Perry. 'They join a new school, the school gives them a bag so that when they go on a trip, they can be recognised as part of the group. If you all have the same bags, it's easier to identify them when you fly or you go on a bus.'

'Why? Why get a special bag? I don't understand the special bag. Girls come with lots of bags.'

Perry continued to walk and watched as Donnie opened up the school building, putting the lights on here and there. He came to the gym. He explained to Perry how the clothes were thrown about. And then he stopped when he reached the cordon, cutting off the admin area. 'What do I do now?' said Donnie. 'I am done. Finished.'

'Have you had your breakfast?' asked Perry.

'Yes,' said Donnie. 'Before I left.'

'Well, I haven't had mine,' said Perry. 'I'm going to get some.'

Perry left Donnie heading back to the janitor's office, while Perry walked over towards the dorms. He kept a fairly discreet distance, not wanting to be seen around dorms at that time. But he passed by the rear of them and saw where there was a wall the campus sat inside of.

Everything about the place was strange because it was old. The wall itself was just a wall. Could you get over it? With a ladder, yes. Too high to jump up and climb over? Donnie said they got out, people coming and going without him knowing how. It was a bit much for the girls to have dug a tunnel. He knew teenagers could be excitable, but this was getting ridiculous.

He thought about what had been said about Georgie Mackie, surprised to get the job, above her level. So why would you put her there? She'd act inappropriately. Surely they must have known a bit of what she was like, albeit she hadn't broken any rules.

I wonder what it is like, living here. You could easily become enclosed, encapsulated, away from everywhere else. There wasn't much around Applecross, after all. Yes, you could go into the town, but how often would they?

Perry wondered whether the town resented the place or not. Did it even notice it? You were paying for an education when you sent your child here. Did they get it? People must have been happy. There were only three hundred girls, after all. It wasn't like an enormous school, but they had special bags. You come in here, put in your dorm, and you have special bags. You're coming and going, the boys from the electricians trying to get in, and someone had got pregnant. Yet there was Mr Kershaw, good-looking Mr Kershaw.

Perry wondered. He felt a tap on his shoulder.

'Hey Perry, you eaten yet?'

'No,' said Perry. 'I don't fancy finding some canteen food either from the school. You think there's something down the road?'

'You'd better be quick. Macleod will be up and on the prowl soon.'

'Come on,' said Perry. 'I'll buy you breakfast.'

Susan stepped in line beside Perry and they walked to the car. He felt it was like they were before but he was worried for her.

Perry knew he'd had to turn her down. He knew he had to be with Tanya and he was happy, but he felt for Susan. Susan needed somebody to depend upon, somebody reliable. She didn't need a man. She just needed a friend. A good friend until she found what she wanted. Perry would try to be a friend to her, and, hopefully, Tanya wouldn't mind. There was a growl in Perry's stomach. He needed to eat badly.

Chapter 08

Alan Ross sat in front of his laptop, staring at the images on the screen. He was linked into the school system, having asked for the records of all the teachers and pupils in the school. It would be a trawl, looking for something that wasn't right, looking for animosity. But as much as he stared at the screen, Alan's mind was working overtime.

Macleod had mentioned that Ross should do the work he was getting Perry and Susan to do. But Ross felt that was unfair. As a sergeant, he understood Hope had always been Macleod's researcher in the field interviewing alongside him. Ross had been a constable then—Macleod's go-to man for setting up the processes, delving into the computer world, looking into things that Macleod couldn't handle. And it had worked well.

Hope had mentioned he was the mum of the team at one point, highlighting the fact that as much as Macleod did the thinking, talked to people, he needed someone to look after him. Someone to make sure everything else occurred around him. Uniform being in the right place at the right time. The assistance requested. The reports from Jona collated. Accommodations booked. The subsistence of the team sorted out as they went far and wide across the highlands and islands.

Ross was good at these things. He was a process man. He wasn't so good at talking to people face to face.

But then he wondered, was he no good? Or was it the fact that the one time he had, the one time he was truly out on his own, it had gone wrong?

It was a while ago on the Monarch Isles. Ross had been stuck there due to the weather, assisted only by a young forensic officer. He had found a drug-making factory hidden away in a gated community and, after investigations, Ross had been shot inside one of the rescue helicopters. Ross didn't know if it was the shooting that made him stay in the background more.

He'd seen colleagues get injured too. Susan had lost a leg. Hope had been nearly kicked to oblivion, almost lost her baby. He'd seen his young son targeted. He also didn't want to be one of those fathers who never came home from work one day. Were these the things that drove him to stay behind the scenes, to stay deep in the online world? In truth, he was good at it, very good at it. This is where his skills lay. He wasn't as good at sussing people out.

That was an annoying fact about Perry. The man looked slovenly. The man didn't look like a police officer. He dressed as if he'd never heard of an iron. There was no smartness to him. And yet, Perry seemed able to decipher people. Even Hope, as much as Ross liked her, didn't conform to the standard way an officer should look in Ross's eyes. She didn't wear a blouse and skirt. She didn't wear trousers, even. It was jeans, a t-shirt, and a leather jacket.

And they called her the pin-up girl. He knew she hated that, and she didn't deserve it. She was more than a pin-up girl. She was a darn fine officer. But she didn't look smart, neat, although she followed the rules more than Macleod ever did.

The back of Ross's mind was rumbling through these things, as the front of it was watching the screen. He was looking through the heads of department, and then the other teachers, and then the pupils. Pupils. Glasgow seemed to come up time and again. Lots of people came from Glasgow. But then again, Applecross wasn't that far away. Glasgow was the nearest. Edinburgh, a city beyond again. Inverness, further up towards the north.

That the school took in people from Glasgow shouldn't have been a shock, especially those on scholarship or assistance. He looked at the heads of department and the other teachers. This was when he noticed something as well. Ross believed in standards. When you got to be a detective, it was because you passed certain exams. You had to go up the ranks proving you were capable of at least knowing what the job involved, and then you had to do it. And in any job, you would sit down and assess the qualifications people had.

The Applecross Academy didn't seem to function in the same way. He looked at interview notes on the teachers' own files. There it stated their strengths and weaknesses in the interview. Qualifications seemed to be glanced over. Ross dug back, as was his way, and pulled in the other applicants for the jobs that the teachers had once applied for and been successful in.

The other applicants at times seem more qualified. Only a few of the teachers came from outside of Glasgow, the rest seemed to have connections back to it. This was all tenuous and in some ways he felt like a conspiracy theorist. There was no evidence, no link, but Ross knew that to establish what it meant the patterns meant was the next stage. Was there anything concrete in what he was looking at?

The joy of a private school, of course, was that they could set up different requirements in their job interviews as opposed to a state school. And so what he was looking at could be simply a school that looks for an original character, a different way of approaching the teaching process. Maybe they wanted people with more experience of the world and fewer who had come simply through the academic route. Comparing files from one to another, applicants to those who were successful, Ross noted that those who got the job, probably wouldn't have got it if this had been a state school. The criteria would have been stricter, more stringent. It was interesting. He wasn't sure whether it was significant.

That being said, they were all of that ilk in the interviews. Especially Georgie Mackie. There were a couple of people with previous headmistress experience. Some of them had taught at private schools as well, not simply state schools. A few of those candidates looked perfect, but Georgie had other qualities, apparently.

Her demeanour and character were highlighted. Highlighted to an extent that Ross wondered how you could do that in such a short interview. Some of the comments about her talked as if they'd known her all their life. Ross stood up from behind the computer, turned and walked over to get a coffee. The little filter machine had done its stuff, and a fresh pot was waiting, from which Ross poured himself a cup. He crouched on the side of one of the desks, sipping his coffee.

Was he in the right place? Hope would come back soon, and then he would have to be the sergeant she wanted. At the end of the day, Macleod, for all he was saying to him, wasn't forcing the issue, because it wasn't his team anymore. He was upstairs. He didn't come with them routinely on investigations. It had taken the Forseti group to involve him last time.

Also, Hope's pregnancy had made Macleod jump in. The investigation had been so big, he had run it from the top. But usually, the murder cases were done by the DI in charge, and that would be Hope. Did Ross fit into Hope's plans? Ever since she'd been in charge, he was struggling, and she was struggling with him; he was sure of it.

The door opened, and Perry ambled in. 'You're not busy then,' he said. 'Pour us a cup.'

Ross glared over at Perry. He had a suit jacket on over a shirt, with a tie hanging off his neck. He looked like he'd been out the previous night. His trousers were held up by a belt that might have been the correct size, but the trouser waist certainly wasn't. Ross could see the bunching where the belt had pulled it tight. He did have good shoes though, Ross noted, but then he was a policeman who'd been on the beat once. If you hadn't learnt the value of good shoes by being on the beat, you'd learnt nothing. Ross turned, took a cup and poured Perry some of the black liquid. Handing it to him, Perry stood for a moment, sipping his coffee.

'Seriously, if you're not busy, could you do something for me?'

'What?' asked Ross.

'I was talking to Donnie. He said something about bags being ordered in. Every time they come here, the girls get a new bag. It's for going away on trips and that. Well, it seems a little unnecessary to me. I don't know how many places you go to that you get bags,' said Perry.

'What if they're all going on school trips? Maybe it's just easier.'

'I don't get it. I mean, seriously? Going along as a group?'

'I don't really see that there's that much to go into here,' said Ross. But he walked over to his laptop, placing his coffee beside it, and then typed. Perry leaned over his shoulder, and Ross could hear him slurp every now and again. The man was classless.

'It's on the invoices here. There are definitely bags being bought. There are repeat orders every year,' said Ross. 'It's true. Every year, they seem to buy a new set of bags. But it's a standard company it's coming from. Look, they order most of their school stuff from there. Uniforms, blouses, it all comes in together. Can't be that much to it.'

'Don't get it. Why would you give them a bag?'

Ross was shaking his head. 'Perry, it's a school bag. They're getting it as part of their uniform.'

'Nobody ever gave me a bag.'

'Did you go to a private school?'

'Well, no,' said Perry. 'But the uniform. Do they pay for the uniform?'

'Part of the fees, apparently,' said Ross. 'When I went through their accounts, the pupils pay to be here. Some are on scholarships. So the uniform comes with it. Apparently, they get measured up, all the details sorted out beforehand. Then they all come in. And the bag is part of that. It's clearly just something that they do. Maybe they send the stuff out in the bag originally.'

'I don't get it. Why would you give a bag? I don't agree with this. You're going to the school. You don't sit and think about, oh, on trips, what shall we do? Do they give them a raincoat? Is that supplied? Is there a standard issue raincoat? Standard issue sou'wester?'

'I think you're overplaying it,' said Ross.

'I could take Susan and talk to the manufacturer, see if that helps,' said Perry.

'No,' said Ross. 'It's not a good use of your time at the moment. Plenty of other things to do. The inspector, no doubt, will have more for you. Anyway, did you learn much from Donnie?'

'Well, I told you, the bag.'

'Anything other than the bag, though,' said Ross, struggling now to maintain an even tone in his voice.

'Donnie thinks there are boys from the electrical company jumping in and out over the back wall, seeing the girls, and that's how the other one got pregnant. He's also not daft. He might be a bit slow, but he's not daft. Donnie reckoned, anyway, that our headmistress wasn't sleeping around. Said she was a bit of a flirt, but not really. And anyway, Donnie doesn't know why they get the bags.'

'You said Donnie was a touch slow.'

'Donnie's slow,' said Perry, 'but Donnie's not stupid. He watches everything, and he didn't understand why the bags were given.'

'I've got to get through some of the rest of this,' said Ross. 'Go and see the inspector. Find out what he wants from you.'

'Of course,' said Perry, quickly drinking his coffee. It took him several goes because it was hot, but when he left the room, Ross almost breathed a sigh of relief. That was the other problem with being a sergeant. You couldn't just get on with your own stuff. You're always there working out what other people need.

The inspector was off to interview James Kershaw, and that would keep him busy for a while. Ross wouldn't need to pick anything up. He'd sent Susan to make sure that Uniform were happy and understood their roles today. All the minutiae, he used to deal with it personally, but now he'd become the ringmaster above that.

He didn't go to deal with things like that; he was expected to interview, talk to, be beside Macleod. But Ross's role, his actual role, was here in front of the computer. Finding out all the information the team couldn't. He was a specialist, really, wasn't he? He didn't know how many sergeants were specialists, though. That was the thing, wasn't it, about running things? You become less and less a specialist. Specialists were brought in.

Jona didn't run things in the investigation. She did her bit and reported on it. She got out of the way. Why couldn't Ross do that? He wished there were specialists on the computing side. Oh, that's right, there were. There were indeed. But that wasn't him either. To be brought in for a bit. He liked the team. He liked being among them. Maybe he needed something else. Hope would be back in a month or two. Or maybe a few more than that, depending what she chose to do.

But when she came back, Ross would need to know what he was doing. He needed to stay in Inverness. He owed that to Angus and his little one. Stability. Maybe Ross could get a job that was more stable. He didn't know of any opportunities though. He gave his head a shake and delved back into his computer.

Chapter 09

Macleod approached the gymnasium, checking his watch to make sure he was on time. Ross had booked a ten o'clock appointment when Macleod would interview James Kershaw. The man had an office at the gymnasium and was indeed waiting for Macleod. James Kershaw was wearing a pair of shorts and a t-shirt with the school crest. He was clearly in very good shape and asked Macleod inside his office. On the walls of the office were several teams of girls ranging from hockey to netball and even a rugby team.

'These are the school teams, are they?' said Macleod.

'Yes,' said Kershaw. 'It's one of the joys to see them compete.'

Macleod looked for a moment, then turned. 'There are only three hundred-odd girls here. Yes?'

'That's correct.'

'Must be difficult pulling the teams together, then. I mean, there can't be that many. I'm sure some girls don't really go in for sports.'

'Oh, they're encouraged to do some sort of sport here. I even teach judo class to some of them. It's good for self-defence.'

'And you taught judo to Georgie Mackie as well.'

Kershaw let his head drop for a moment. 'I'm so sorry she's gone. Don't get me wrong. Georgie was a lovely person.'

'You got to know her well then through the judo.'

'Yes, obviously. I mean, I was never on my own with Georgie in the judo. But I was with her, as well as Lily, Mia and Iris. Georgie was good at judo. She enjoyed it. I think it was her way of letting go, of getting some time away. It's difficult running a school.'

'She was quite young for a headmistress, wasn't she?' said Macleod.

'Yes, but she was good. She knew what she was doing.'

'She was also provocative,' ventured Macleod.

'Modern, I would have said. The thing about Georgie was she was needed. Our deputy headmistress would keep the school in the past. I'm all for standards,' said James, 'but you have to move forward. Girls don't behave like they did forty, fifty years ago. A modern woman dresses how she wants. Georgie showed them they should have confidence in that.'

'She also seemed to attract criticism for sunbathing in her garden, on view to the rest of them.'

'That's just fuddy-duddy nonsense,' said James.

'Were you in any way linked to Georgie beyond the teaching relationship?'

'Well, I said we were, hopefully, good colleagues, friends to a point. But if you're asking, was there anything beyond that? No.'

'Well,' said Macleod, 'we have heard rumours about you. Now, they may just be rumours. I'm not putting any stock in them yet. I'm just asking you formally—was there anything? If so, now's the time to say it.'

'I can't help it, Inspector, if women think I'm attractive. I don't encourage them, though. That's the difference.'

'Did Georgie think you were attractive?'

'We could mutually appreciate each other,' said James, and Macleod wondered what he meant by that.

'Did you find her attractive?'

'Well, Georgie was attractive. The thing is, Pauline's the one who's watched me.'

'Pauline Drummond? You're saying that Pauline Drummond has been, what?'

'Ogling me; she stares at me all the time.'

'Really? She doesn't seem the sort; she seems to be—'

'Yes, I know what she seems to be, but I think the woman protests too much; that's what they say, isn't it? She's constantly looking at me. In fact, I remember an incident—maybe I shouldn't say.'

'Go on.'

'Well, the thing is, Inspector, I was in my changing room. Obviously, being male, one of the few male staffers, we don't have large facilities. There's a shower behind my changing room; it's a small one. There's usually only me who uses it. Donnie's about. You get the occasional other male teacher or staff member. But we have a small changing area for us. The girls' ones are much bigger, as well as another small one for the female staff.'

'Go on,' said Macleod.

'Well, I was having a shower, and I stepped out, and I was drying myself down. I looked up, and Pauline Drummond had walked into my changing room.'

'What did you do?'

'I didn't say anything,' said James. 'My towel was behind my back and she wasn't embarrassed. She just stood there, staring at me. In fact, I think she was enjoying it.'

'She was looking at you, and you were looking back.'

'No, I had my eyes closed. I often do when I dry down my back. But yes, she stood there. Might have been a good part of a minute before she made herself known to me. She gave a cough.'

'And what? Stepped out.'

'No, you'd have thought that, wouldn't you? Well, in fact, you'd have thought she wouldn't have coughed at all. She'd have just stepped out. But no, she coughed and she stared for another couple of seconds, making sure I'd seen her.' James smirked. 'Obviously, she liked what she saw.'

Macleod struggled to rationalise this. The woman in the teachers' common room had been actively against that sort of thing. That she'd stayed, and she continued to watch, and more than that, she'd actually coughed, bringing James's attention to being there, was hard to rationalise. Of course, it was James's view of the proceedings. Was it accurate? Was it just a made-up fantasy to throw Macleod off the trail? He wasn't sure.

'But you and Georgie had no such a circumstance, or indeed Iris or any of the rest of them.'

'Pauline was jealous of us for the judo. It was fun. Have you ever been with some women and having fun? Nothing out of hand. But you know, the odd cheeky comment.'

Macleod shook his head. That wasn't him. It wasn't what he did, and certainly back in the day it wasn't something that would have been done.

'Georgie liked the odd comment about her from me. Maybe Pauline's jealous of that. Pauline wouldn't take part in the judo. She wasn't as fit as Georgie.'

'I take it you appreciate a woman who is fit,' said Macleod.

James looked bemused. 'Well, I think we all do, Inspector, don't we?'

Macleod nodded, more to just accept the comment, rather than to actually agree with it. He wondered. 'Can you think of anybody else?' asked Macleod, 'who'd have a reason for dispatching Georgie in this way.'

'No,' said James. 'Georgie was lovely and a thoroughly good headmistress. Georgie was fun. The woman was a wonderful influence on the girls. One thing Georgie was not, was a slut. If I can be candid, Inspector.'

Macleod thought he'd already been candid, but he nodded anyway.

'Georgie as a partner? As a young man, would I have liked to have got close to Georgie? Would I have liked to have got her into bed? Well, of course. But Georgie wasn't like that. She was no slut.'

'Somebody thought so,' said Macleod. 'Somebody thought it enough that they actually set up a tableau when they killed her. That tends to be someone with an idea of vengeance, of holding somebody up for what they truly are.'

'Or somebody who's pretty sick in the mind,' said James. 'I'm telling you now, Georgie was not like that. Georgie was a good influence. I'm very sorry that she's dead because she was a friend. Very much a friend,' said James, becoming quiet.

'Did she have anyone here that she had problems with? Anyone who was blocking maybe her agenda for the school? Maybe they were—'

'Georgie was difficult for some of the older ones to accept,' said James. 'But they accepted it. Mrs Fotheringham-Smythe, she's not daft. She realised that the school needed a younger influence. Someone to bring the girls forward. And yes, there was an uneasy tension at times between them. But she brought Georgie in. She was one of the ones who said yes. So, for her to die like this, it makes little sense to me. Really makes little sense. If Georgie was up to things like that, she'd hide it very well because she was not stupid,' said James.

Macleod could hear a commotion inside the office.

'What's that?' he asked.

'That's my class arriving. It's netball. I'll need to take them in five or ten minutes. Just a second.' James jumped up out of his chair, went over to the door, opened it, and shouted out into the corridor beside the gymnasium. 'Girls, just go on ahead and get changed and get going in the gym. Okay? I'm just speaking to the inspector at the moment. Go in and warm up.'

'I don't wish to keep you back,' said Macleod. 'In fact, I think that'll be enough for now.' Macleod stood up from his chair. As he turned, he noticed again the pictures on the wall. There were girls in various sports outfits.

'What are these ones? As opposed to the teams.'

'That's some girls who have done well in the sports. They won prizes.'

'National?' asked Macleod.

'No, here. I select the prize each year. The girls in each year who have done the best.'

Macleod looked at the girls in their sportswear. Something was bothering him about James Kershaw. Macleod decided to observe him. So he turned and shook the man's hand before leaving the office.

The sports hall had a balcony above it, and Macleod made his way up to it. He took a seat and sat down close to the edge of the balcony but just far enough back so he could just see over the top. He was in the shade and thought he would struggle to be seen.

Sitting there as the girls ran out warming up for their netball, he watched James as the girls surrounded him in a half circle. He encouraged them, talking about what they would do today in their netball. A small match ensued, and Macleod watched James.

His eyes were everywhere, and every now and again, they would settle on one girl. She had black hair and a ponytail, and for her age, she was very good-looking and toned. But James seemed to look at her much more than the others, but he also looked at the others in a way that Macleod recognised.

He sat back for a moment, making sure he was definitely not visible to the court below. Macleod knew what it was for a good-looking woman to walk past you, and your head to be turned. It was the animal instinct, the one most men had. Maybe some women had it too. He wasn't one to venture into that discussion in the company of a mixed group.

But that was where it ended. You saw them go past; you moved on. That was the animal side of a person. Inbuilt, that you would find the best mate, keep the species going. James Kershaw, however, looked again and again beyond that. He needed a second opinion.

Macleod sent a text message to Perry, telling him to quietly enter the gymnasium and advised where he was. Five minutes later, Perry appeared on the balcony and carefully looked down at the court below when told by Macleod to watch James Kershaw. After a few minutes, Macleod indicated they should leave the gymnasium and step outside.

'What did you make of Mr Kershaw?' asked Macleod.

'Certainly involved in his teaching.'

'Perry. Assessment. What were you thinking about him? Everything. Just tell me. Don't hold back.'

'Well, he certainly likes that black-haired girl, doesn't he? The one with the ponytail. Doesn't take his eyes off her.'

'More so than a lot of the rest of them. Do you think he was watching her from an athletic point of view?'

'No,' said Perry. 'I know what he was watching her for. Enjoying himself.'

'That's what I thought. Susan also made that comment at our meeting. One of the girls said he was a pervert. We've got a pregnant young girl as well in town.'

'You don't think that's all connected do you? That's a bit of an extrapolation.'

'It is,' said Macleod, 'but I have been told that Georgie Mackie was not a slut although the murderer said that. There may be more going on. A murderer saying that our headmistress was getting about with other people. James is one of the few men here. Donnie?'

'Wasn't getting about with Donnie,' said Perry. 'Nice lad, slow but clever and no, definitely not getting about with Donnie.'

'So, who's she getting about with? There's few here to do that with except James. Maybe the electricians, the boys coming over the wall. That said our murderer is sending us to the gym with the scattered clothes. Or . . .'

'Or what?' asked Perry.

'I don't know,' said Macleod. 'Maybe something else entirely.'

Chapter 10

Jona Nakamura was packing up the last of her forensic wagon. It had been a long haul as ever. By the time they'd closed off the scene, got the body sorted, checked through with all their processes—and then have the inspector march all over it and start demanding answers how the unfortunate woman had died—Jona got little rest.

She always found it funny that the detectives complained, yet they could step aside, sit and have their coffee. They went here and there. The forensic team arrived and just went full at it, knowing they had to complete their procedures quickly. Luckily, this death happened inside. They weren't fighting against the rain with temporary shelters.

That being said, Jona had been working hard for the last forty-eight hours. And now, she was ready to head back up the road. Before she would though, she was going to take a short stroll.

Jona had seen little of the grounds, and she certainly didn't want to march into the school buildings. So, she headed off towards a set of buildings off to one side. She didn't know what they were for, but there were greenhouses and other buildings. There was little in the greenhouses, and there was no one about, so Jona thought this would be perfect. Somewhere to get away from it all.

Jona would go there, sit down and do her contemplation, her meditation, away from everyone. She couldn't do it by the wagon, because they'd come looking for her. Always, somebody from the team came to ask a question. At least she was away from there. If the phone would go, she could see who it would be.

If it were Robbie, she'd know to leave the answer. Robbie was always asking questions, always wanting verification. The others could just get on with things. It wasn't Robbie's fault. He'd been burned in a previous unit. Been told that he'd overstepped the mark. Not by Jona, but by his previous boss. And now Robbie wanted confirmation of everything.

The weather was blustery, and as Jona got close to the greenhouses, she realised they were truly empty, or rather, stripped. There was nothing inside—not a single plant—nothing. She stepped inside one; the door was hanging awkwardly.

Looking at the door, it seemed in reasonably good nick. It was hanging open, but it wasn't hanging loose. In fact, this could simply be shut up if required. She stepped inside the greenhouse, and it looked in good condition. There certainly wasn't months of growth. It was almost as if, well, as if it was ready for use, had been used and simply everything had been removed.

Jona was good at these sorts of things. It's what she noticed. There should have been, if this had been left for a while, moss growing, lichen, fungus, some sign or other. Wildlife always found a way to grow back over what was left. Leave a piece of wood in the grass, and the grass grew over it and eventually the wood disappears. Similarly, life would grow inside here. It might be lichen, it might be moss, it might be mushrooms in the darker recesses. Something, some spore would travel in, take hold and grow and develop. Life worked.

The wind, however, would be a problem to her meditating. Even with that door closed, she would hear it howling around the edge of these greenhouses. She stepped out, walked past another greenhouse, but then made for the brick buildings.

Again, the door was open, but it wasn't hanging loose. It was open. As she stepped inside, she thought it was remarkably clean. Over time, with the door open, animals would get in, maybe the odd rat, mice, something. Insects would find their way through too. These floors were fairly clean.

She looked up at the electrical connections. They were still intact . There were hooks where pipework would have been. The pipework was gone, but the brackets for it were there. Looking at those brackets, pipework would have run across the room. There were hooks that would have held something else. *It was like, well, what was it like?* she asked herself.

Jona crouched down for a moment, staring. She was working in the light that was flooding in from the open door. So, she turned to one of the switches and flicked it. Light came on. Jona traced the electrical connections. Outside the building was a fuse box. She flicked it open. There were several fuses there. Some seemed quite large.

Why would you need such a large fuse box for a place like this? Jona wondered and then turned, seeking the next building. Again, the door was open, and inside was similar. The floor was tiled, and it was in good shape. There was nothing on the walls, no posters, nothing from before, and yet there were still the fixtures that would have held pipes. The fixtures that would have held something else. *Maybe lights? Is that what it was?*

The basic lights were there. But were there other lights? she wondered. *If you closed the door to the room, you could maintain the temperature.* She looked up at the ceiling. It would be hard to get up there, for Jona was only short. Hope might have been able to touch the ceiling with a jump. She wondered, because it was a false ceiling, was there something else up there? Insulation? There was a roof above it.

All thoughts of meditation had left Jona's mind, and she walked on to a third building. As she approached it, she thought she heard noises. Carefully, she crept forward. There were two voices, both young women, from the sounds of it.

'Can't believe she was found like that. Imagine it.'

'You think that inspector enjoyed it when he saw her?'

'Get out! It'd be disgusting. She's dead.'

'Yeah, that's a pity. I mean, she was good, wasn't she? Do you remember that time they caught her sunbathing? They were all complaining about it. That was funny. That James Kershaw, though. He was there the whole time.'

'He's always there. He's always there when you can see anything. I had him for PE when we were on the bikes and the treadmills, and he stood there watching. He stood behind us all. I swear he's looking at all our bums.'

'Yeah, he's a bit of a perv, isn't he? He's nice, though. Would you fancy it with him?'

'I think I would. Do you think he's hung?'

'Well, I think—'

The voice stopped as Jona walked into the room. The smell of cigarette smoke had prompted Jona to walk in. These were clearly two girls hiding away, and now they would be caught, but not by a teacher, but by someone from outside.

They were sitting in school uniforms, backs up against the wall, chatting, cigarettes in their mouths. Jona understood the picture straightaway. Of course they were out here, far away. Anything to get a cigarette and not be seen.

The girls went to get up and flee, but Jona held up her hand. 'It's okay. Stop,' she said. 'I'm Jona Nakamura. I'm a forensic officer with the police. You have nothing to fear from me. But you really should stop smoking those.'

One girl turned and put her cigarette out beside her, but the other continued to puff. 'There's nothing wrong with it. Tastes good.'

'They'll kill you in the long run. You'll choke and you'll cough. You'll splutter. And you'll be unfit.'

'Yeah, well. It won't matter when you have a baby, will it?'

'Tell me about these places,' said Jona.

'Why,' said the girl. 'Why would we tell you anything?'

'Because I'm the forensic officer with the police. And if you don't, I will ask your deputy headmistress what you're doing here and find out from her about these places. But you'll be dropped in it. On the other hand, you can talk to me quietly. The other thing is that I might have to bring over my inspector to talk to you. He asks very different questions.'

'All right,' said the girl who'd put her cigarette out. 'What do you want to know?'

'These buildings, greenhouses outside, have they always been like this. Door open.'

'Hell no,' said the girl with the fag. 'This here? You couldn't get in here weeks ago. Not that many weeks ago either. All locked up. Asked Donnie about it.'

'The janitor.'

80

'Yeah. He's all right, Donnie. Nice man. Slow, simple. Nice man. Doesn't look at your arse like that James Kershaw does.'

'What did Donnie say about these buildings?' asked Jona.

'Donnie said they just had to be kept locked up. Donnie hadn't been in them.'

'What about the greenhouses? Did you see anything in there?'

'There were plants in the greenhouse, but you couldn't get near them. They were locked up too. If you were seen around here, you got told to go away from them. They told us they weren't safe, these buildings.'

Jona looked around the room they were in. They seemed perfectly safe to her.

'Why? What was wrong with them?'

'Asbestos. What we were told.'

'Asbestos?' said Jona.

'There was a false ceiling up there. Some people came and ripped the whole place out.'

'What about the greenhouses?'

'They were unstable. But there were plants growing in them. They were using them for stuff.'

'Really?' said Jona.

'Yes, these people came in and took the stuff away. Apparently in the night. We never saw it. But then we came by and the doors were open. We had a look and there was nothing here. It's difficult to get a cigarette around here. To get away.'

'So you thought you'd come here because nobody else would come here, because it was all locked up before, wasn't it?'

'Exactly,' said the girl. 'Come and have your fag in peace. Nobody to complain at you, nobody to shout. In fact, till you came, we'd seen no one.'

'I'm going to make you a deal,' said Jona. 'You keep quiet about meeting me here, and I'll keep quiet about you.'

'Deal,' said the girl with the cigarette. Jona looked at the one behind her, who had put hers out.

'Deal.'

'Good,' said Jona. But she watched as the girl without a cigarette now reached into her jacket and pulled out another packet. She pulled the cigarette out and lit up.

'Seriously, though,' said Jona, 'you need to quit. You get hooked on them now, you don't get off them. Besides, how can you afford them? They're so expensive now.'

'So what do you have us do?'

'Meditate?'

'What? Just sit and think? I have to sit and think all day long in those classrooms.'

'Are you not missing from a class though?'

'We don't have class all the time,' said the girl. 'Sometimes you have free periods. You can do other things, like go to the gym or that. But I'm not going into the gym. I hate James Kershaw sitting watching my arse.'

'Well, my colleague said that he was a pervert. At least one of the other girls had said it. Is he really?'

'All the girls love him. Well, how he looks. But he is. He never stops staring, but he has his favourites, you know. Some of them win sports prizes. But, it's not a sports prize, is it? It's best legs. I've been in his office and I've seen them. You go left to right, you know. It's a different award. It's not what it says underneath. It's not about being the best hockey player. It's not about that. Best legs.'

'That's right, that's Amy. Best legs. And Frauke, the German lass. You know what that's about.'

The other girl jumped in. 'Yeah. Best boobs.'

'OK,' said Jona. 'I think I get the idea. Get off the cigarettes, though.'

She turned and left and then stood outside for a moment. The girls inside were quiet, and then they began their talk again. It had gone back to the death of Georgie Mackie and the rumours surrounding it. Jona left them, but as she walked back towards her wagon, she thought about the greenhouses.

They'd been full of plants. You wouldn't get asbestos in those buildings. That didn't make sense. She'd need to tell Macleod about this. Clearly, something was up. Donnie didn't know. Donnie had told the girls. The place had been locked, and now the places were open; they looked perfectly usable; there'd been fixtures.

Jona wondered, *what could you have in there? What could you grow? Or were things being stored? Were things being produced? What was it?* Jona would need to tell Macleod and then get up the road. She had a body to look at on the slab and a long drive before that.

Chapter 11

Susan parked the car on the side of the street. Applecross was not an enormous place, more a small village, but the building she was looking at was smart. It looked like a new build, and Susan thought she could make out four flats within it. She jumped out of the car, joining Perry, whom she'd driven into town with.

'That one there,' said Perry.

'Yes,' said Susan. 'New build by the looks of it. Looks quite smart if out of place. Let's see who Keira Saunders is, then.'

'I wonder if she's heard about the headmistress.'

'A place like this, a school attached to it, you bet. Word will have got down all over the village.'

'I suppose so,' said Perry. 'We had some press around too.'

They walked along a smart pathway and then rang a buzzer, one of four on the front door.

'Hello?' said a young woman's voice.

'Hi, this is the police. DC Perry and DC Cunningham. We'd like to have a word, if that's possible. Would you be Keira Saunders?'

'Yes. Hang on. I'll come down.'

'We understand you're pregnant? It's okay; we can come up.

You are on the top floor, aren't you?'

'That's correct.'

A buzzer went, Susan tried the door, and it opened. Together they climbed the stairs and found a woman standing at the door of a flat. She was certainly pregnant, although Susan would have said maybe six to seven months. She was showing, but not massively.

'Keira Saunders?' asked Susan.

'That's correct. How can I help you?'

'Well, it would be possible to step inside for a moment. It's just something that's happened up at the school we'd like to talk to you about.'

'Okay,' said Keira. The woman was lean, with long legs and long black hair. Despite her pregnancy, she looked athletic. She was also quite buxom.

Susan and Perry followed Keira inside, where she sat down on a seat. She had leggings on, which seemed to have an elastic waist. On top, she wore a crop top with an open shirt over it. She sat on the edge of her seat, her hands between her legs and Perry thought she looked quite nervous.

'Have you heard about the developments up at the school?' asked Susan.

'The headmistress is dead. I heard she was killed.'

'Who did you hear that from?' asked Perry.

'The word's out in the village. And the papers are reporting it too. Is it not accurate?'

'I'm afraid the headmistress was murdered,' said Susan. Keira put her hand up to her mouth. She looked shocked, and some tears formed.

'Did you know Georgie Mackie well?'

'The headmistress was very kind to me. And she helped me

get the flat I'm in now. When I found out I was pregnant, she was very understanding.'

'You were at the school at the time?' asked Perry.

'That's right. I had gone there from Glasgow. I'd managed to get a scholarship. Lucky, really, because we didn't have that much at home. I grew up on an estate in Glasgow. And then I'd gone to this school. It was wonderful. They help you develop your intellect. And then, well, I made a mistake.'

'You view it as a mistake,' said Susan, 'the child you're going to have.'

'I made a mistake in not making sure that we would end up not having a child,' said Keira. 'I was infatuated. It just, well, we just, we just did it one night, and I realised the next day too late we hadn't, well, we hadn't been careful.'

'And who was the father?' asked Perry. Suddenly, Keira began to cry, and Susan shot Perry a look, but Perry thought it was a question that needed to be asked even though he knew the answer.

'I'm sorry,' she said. 'Max. Max is the father, but Max is dead.'

'I'm so sorry,' said Susan. 'Was he a local lad?'

'Max worked at the electrician's. He was a likeable lad. Yeah, he treated me very well.'

'Does it happen a lot? You girls going with the boys from the electricians,' said Susan.

'The school doesn't know how to stop it. There are ways out of those grounds if you know what you're doing,' said Keira. 'I knew what I was doing with getting out of the school. Obviously, I didn't know what I was doing when I ended up getting pregnant.'

'You said that Max was no longer with us,' said Perry. 'What happened?'

'It was an accident. The vehicle hit him. He was on his motorbike. But the driver drove off, leaving him. He died there. On the road. It's hard to take. Hard to take that somebody would just do that.'

'Absolutely,' said Susan. 'That's terrible. Truly. I'm very sorry.'

'If you don't mind my asking, why are you here? If you've got a home and Max is no longer here, why wouldn't you go back to the estate and go back to your parents? Wouldn't they be able to support you more?' asked Perry.

'No,' said Kiera. 'The trouble is that, well, they've disowned me. When I got pregnant, they said that was that. Kicked me out. Said not to bother coming home. That's why the headmistress was so kind. She got me this flat. I've got to now make a life up here, haven't I? She'd said that when the baby came, they'd talk about what they could offer me, work-wise and things. But I don't know what'll happen now if she's not there.'

'How are you coping?' asked Perry.

'Well, I get by, I eat. I get myself about here and there. The school has been quite good. The headmistress made sure I'm okay.'

'You're going to need to work at some point, though, aren't you?' said Perry.

'Once the baby's come, then we can look at that.'

'You didn't think about it? Working now? Then you would have the chance to put something aside. I'm no expert with babies, but I understand some women work maybe until they're eight months.'

'I'm not sure I could. The baby takes more out of you than

you think,' said Kiera. 'Well, after it's born, yes, I probably have to think about that.'

'Do Max's parents help at all?'

'No,' said Kiera. 'They weren't thrilled with him either. Max was helping. He was very good, but now he's gone.'

'How did you find the school?' asked Perry, changing the subject.

'I was very happy. They've got everything there.'

'Indeed,' said Perry. 'When you got your scholarship, did that mean you got all your uniform as well? Did the—'

'Yes. Yes, the scholarship paid for all of that,' said Keira, bemused at the change in direction of questioning. 'They paid for my time there. It's incredibly generous. I can't believe I messed it up so bad.'

'And the teaching, was it good? Were you looking to go on and do what?'

'I would have got my highers. Maybe gone off to university. I can't do that now. Might get back, I guess. Afterwards, they may let me come back and study up there. It was all very open. I guess we'll see who the new headmistress is, or headmaster. Maybe they'll see it different to how Miss Mackie saw it.'

'I guess,' said Perry. 'It's just something you'll have to see about. When you got your uniform, though,' he said, 'did you get a bag with it?'

'Oh, yes. You get a bag.'

'One with a school emblem on it, a logo?'

'Yes,' said Keira.

'Why?' asked Perry. 'What's it for?'

'For going away on trips. They do quite a lot of trips. Down to Glasgow. Sometimes to Edinburgh. Sometimes up to Inverness. Not big trips on planes away to foreign places.

But they thought it was important to get us out to museums, to other cultural events. They'd also got us to go to the theatre. It's a little bit of free time down in the city. A lot of us are from cities and, well, Applecross here doesn't really cut it as a lively place.'

'I can get that,' said Perry. 'I used to be in Glasgow. Was there for quite a while, actually. This seems rather remote.'

'Thinking back about the headmistress,' said Susan, 'can you think of any reason anyone would want to see her dead?'

'Oh, no. Most of the girls loved her. She was very forward-thinking. Even in the way she dealt with me, progressive—that's what they say about her, you know? And she dressed like we dress today, too. The deputy headmistress took a very dim view when I got pregnant. But the headmistress helped me, sorted me out. The deputy head, she said I had brought the school into disrepute.'

'Did Miss Drummond have anything to say as well?'

'Preppy Pauline,' said Keira.

'Pauline Drummond,' confirmed Perry.

'Yes, Pauline Drummond. Preppy Pauline, that's what they called her. Oh, she was always so eggy.'

'Can I ask you something else?' said Perry. 'There was a teacher there who took PE, James Kershaw. Did you know him?'

'We all knew him. He took everyone for PE at some point or other.'

'Some girls described him as a pervert. Would you say that?'

'No,' said Kiera, almost like she was in another place. 'He was quite, well, gorgeous. He had an impressive body on him. Very charming. Very charming, but the body was something else. He could persuade anyone into anything, I think.'

'Well, a lot of the girls have said he's watching them all the time.'

'Yes. I guess it must be hard for a young man, all of us running around. They say that, don't they? That's the thing, isn't it? How does a male schoolteacher survive with these young bodies running around?' giggled Kiera.

'I'd have thought if he talked to them,' said Perry, 'he'd probably be desperate to get out of there.'

Susan looked across at Perry, glaring at him as if he'd said something wrong.

'Not that there's anything wrong with teenage girls. I just think if you get a large group of them together, an older man is just not going to be that interested. His head's going to be done in with what he will see is as babble and other sorts of things,' said Perry.

'James wasn't that old, and he was very good-looking,' said Kiera.

'Well, thank you for your time,' said Susan. 'We appreciate it.' She stood up, and Perry followed. They made their way back to the car.

'That was interesting, wasn't it? Her parents disowned her. Georgie was looking after her.'

'Very interesting. Who pays the rent?' asked Perry. 'Who pays for food, subsistence? Who keeps her in the lifestyle she's accustomed to? That is not a cheap flat. That is not somebody who's scraped by into a council place. It's someone being looked after, so somebody is paying all the bills at that place, not just the rent.'

'Maybe, but to get accommodation, that's good,' said Susan. 'I would be scared being up here on my own. No family. You're pregnant. It must be petrifying for her, unless somebody's looking after her. At least she's got good accommodation. At least she's somewhere where she's got a chance.'

'Did you notice something, though?' asked Perry.

'What?'

'No photos. There were no photos of Max. In fact, there were very few photos at all. I saw one, though.'

'Yes,' said Susan. 'You mean the one that was over in the corner? It was her, wasn't it? It was Keira, in a sports outfit.'

'It was an award. She had won an award from the school to do with sports. I think it said best gymnast.'

'What about it? She's got a best gymnast award from the school.'

'I was talking to Macleod earlier. James Kershaw, he watches the girls. He watches certain girls in that way that says he's not just being a PE teacher. He's watching them to enjoy. Some of them.'

'And?' said Susan.

'And he does the awards for the best this and that. Seems strange to me.'

'Are you saying he just gives the awards to the ones he likes the best?'

'Just a thought. What I do know is, no photographs of Max. Not sure who's paying the bills. We need to look into this further.'

'Well, I can agree with that,' said Susan.

Chapter 12

'I'm about to get on the way, but I thought I should see you first.'

'Okay,' said Macleod. 'Why?' He was currently making his way back from a tour of the school. He wanted to see where everyone was, how they went about their normal business. Perry had gone off with Susan into town to see the girl who had got pregnant, and Ross was buried deep in his laptop as ever.

'You weren't easy to find, and I need to be up the road, Seoras,' said Jona. 'But look, I was out near the buildings that don't get used much. The other side of the campus.'

'Okay,' said Macleod. 'What about them?'

'Have you been into any of them? Have you had a look?'

'No, they were just buildings that were locked up.'

'They were locked up. They're not locked up anymore.'

'But Perry said that Donnie wasn't that interested in them. It wasn't part of his remit, it wasn't—'

'They're wide open. I caught two girls in there smoking.'

'Well, that's not unusual. It's a school, after all. Teenagers. Some of them are bound to be trying to get a cig,' said Macleod.

'I wouldn't be bringing that to you, would I?' said Jona.

'Outside, there are three greenhouses. They look like they've been emptied quickly. They look like they've just been abandoned. But it's not been that long. They haven't had time to have anything grow back, for the wild to take over. Similarly with the buildings. According to the girls, they used to be locked up tight. Nobody could get in. Donnie didn't even go in. But now they're wide open. And they look like they've been cleared.'

'Cleared?' mused Macleod.

'Cleared,' said Jona. 'When you strip stuff out, sometimes they leave behind the brackets. The things that would hold stuff. So it looks like there was a load of pipework in there. It looks like things were hung from the ceiling. But while everything's stripped out, the main lights are still there. Why? Why would you do that?

'The floor is also clean. They have had little growth come back. The girls said that they had been told there was asbestos in there. Difficult to believe. There's a false ceiling. We wouldn't have asbestos up there. It would have been done by now if they ever had any. Long time ago. It just doesn't make sense to me. I think there used to be something in there, and it was locked up. Maybe it was something people didn't want to be seen.'

'Thank you,' said Macleod. 'It certainly warrants further investigation. I'll look into that. You have a good trip up.'

'I'll get a proper look at the body. Confirm what I think. Are you sure you can do without me for the rest of this?'

'I'm never sure of anything,' said Macleod. 'But hey, safe trip. Will you see Hope in the next couple of days? Give her my best. I won't be around to see the wee man.'

'She said you're around quite a bit.'

93

'Well, she named him after me.'

'You never had children, did you?' said Jona.

'No,' said Macleod, 'and he's not my grandchild. He's just Hope's child. Hope's and John's.'

'But he's your godchild.'

'Yes, he is,' said Macleod, smiling. Jona turned away to her car and Macleod made his way back to the little office that had been set up for the team. Inside the room, he saw Ross once again sitting in front of his laptop.

'You need to get out and do some more legwork,' he said. 'Get out and see the place. You need to get a feel for what's going on. That might be why you don't seem to pick up on certain things that I do, Ross.'

'With respect,' said Ross, 'you sit in front of a laptop and are clueless.'

'That's not what I'm saying. You need to do the legwork.'

'Susan and Perry can do that. It's what they're good at. I'm fine here.'

'Hope might change that when she comes back. As long as you're aware of that. And it'll be her call. She'll be running it. Hope decides what sort of sergeant she wants. She decides how the team operates.'

'I'm aware of that,' said Ross.

'Anyway, can you look into something for me? There are outbuildings on the far side of the school. They are empty, but they were cleared at some point. Can you look into the records and see when they were cleared and why they were cleared? See if there're any bills or that with them?'

'Yes, I will do it but there's something more important first.'

'More important,' said Macleod. 'What?'

'I've been looking into the background of the school, the

interviews done with staff. I've found that staff here wouldn't have been hired by the state schools. Because of the vetting process they have to go through and the points awarding, state schools have to give it to the most evidenced person, not necessarily who you think,' said Ross. 'Whereas the private schools they don't follow the same procedure. They have greater flexibility. A lot of the teachers working here wouldn't be working here if this were a state school.'

'So private schools and state schools are different,' said Macleod. 'How does it help me?'

'Well, I said, there's something else I've been looking into. I looked at the finances, and the school goes on a lot of trips during the year. The trips are mainly to Glasgow, Edinburgh, and Inverness. I thought that was unusual, but then again, it's school trips.' Macleod nodded. 'So I decided I would cross-reference the timing of the trips, and I've looked at it regarding things reported by the police. Now, seventy per cent of them match with drug officers reporting shipments arriving in these various cities.'

'So you're telling me that seven out of ten times a school trip arrives when there's a drug deal being made. I mean, how often are drug deals being made? What are you suggesting? Schoolkids are all just piling down with a ton of gear?'

'It could be a coincidence. I accept that,' said Ross, 'because there's no direct link. It's an extrapolation by the computer, but something doesn't feel right,' said Ross.

'Have you passed it on to the drug teams down in the various cities?'

'Yes,' said Ross, 'but again I've told them it might just be a coincidence.'

'Good. You may need to tighten it up if this is the line you're taking, and you want to prove it. You're going to have to go further than that. I'm not sure it is worth following up, but if you can do it quickly and not cause you too much hassle, and certainly not put anything else in the case to detriment, then by all means,' said Macleod.

'Okay,' said Ross. 'I'll get on it.'

'Get on those buildings too, but do it quietly, okay? Nobody knows we know anything about them at the moment. Jona got it from a couple of schoolgirls who were smoking, so they'll be keen that nobody knows they were in there.'

'I'll get on it,' said Ross.

'Check Donnie. Donnie might be an excellent source of information. Apparently, he never actually went inside any of these places. But Donnie seems to walk around everywhere, so he might know a bit more about them than he lets on initially.'

'Will do,' said Ross.

'And Ross, put some more legwork in, okay? I'm thinking of you, Alan. You've struggled since you moved up to sergeant. I'm not even sure you want the sergeant's job.'

'My situation at home changed. We have a little one. We have—'

'I get it, I get it,' said Macleod.

'No, you don't,' said Ross suddenly. Macleod stepped back. It was unlike Ross to say such a thing to the inspector.

'You constantly say you understand this, you understand that. How can you? You've never had kids, never been woken up in the middle of the night. You've never had your partner telling you they need time off and you need to cover. Never had them complain to you when you're away night after night after night trying to find some damn killer. And it keeps you away from all the little things, from taking the wee guy here, the wee guy there. Angus doesn't get out to other things. He's trapped then. Do you get it? No, you don't. You don't. Not with a woman at home cooking your meals when you come in. You haven't got a child depending on you.'

'Well, you're right,' said Macleod. 'I don't probably understand it fully. I do understand being away. That I do. Do you understand Jane needing me to be back home? But no, I don't understand it with kids. But at the end of the day, Alan, we need you to do your job as a detective sergeant. I don't like to say this, because I think you're good for the team. I think you're good at what you do. But if it doesn't suit family life, there are plenty of other roles within the force. Maybe you should look at them.

'There's no point you going on like this. You're just getting angry, crabby at people. The situation is yours to resolve, not the force's. The detective sergeant job requires certain things. A certain flexibility with your time and commitments is one of them. Now, I believe you know that. Your problem at the moment is you're not making a decision, a choice.'

'My problem at the moment is I don't have time to make the choice. We're here, we're there, we're everywhere. Last time we had threats to our family. You don't get that either, do you?'

'Now that's not fair,' said Macleod. 'My own Jane was nearly put into an acid bath at one point.'

'But you haven't had a wee man threatened. You haven't had the little pride and joy of your life threatened. Jane chose to be there. Jane chose to stand by you. He didn't. He's an innocent. And we did not protect him enough. That's the problem. He shouldn't have this disruption. He should have his father there with him. I mean, you're his godparent. Maybe you should think about that.'

97

Macleod wasn't quite sure what that comment meant, but Ross was clearly incensed.

'I'll let you be,' said Macleod. 'But it's clearly agitating you. Keep going with what you're doing.'

Macleod stepped out of the office. He needed to sit and think, but he would not sit in there. Not with the way Ross had just exploded. He was glad he hadn't exploded back at him. An earlier version of himself would have done. Not now. Now, he knew what this job was. He knew how it took it out of you, even if you didn't have kids. So he couldn't blame Ross for his feelings. But he needed to decide. He needed to be in or out.

And there were plenty of other jobs. You could still be a detective with some of them. The trouble with the murder squad was it happened, and you went, and you stayed until it was done. Or until at least there was nothing else to find out in that location.

Some of the other jobs were better. The cold case files, for instance. Often you just didn't go anywhere with those. A lot of time was spent at the office. Even the arts world stuff. That rarely required much time spent away. It was closer to home.

Yes, you were popping out to different things, and you had to understand the arts world, which Ross, as far as Macleod understood, didn't. He'd also have to work with Clarissa. Macleod thought back to the pair of them working together. 'Als' she had called him. The trouble with Clarissa was that she was a prickly customer if you weren't used to her, or you couldn't get used to her. She relented to no one.

Macleod sat down on a bench in a grassy part of the grounds. He was going to pull out his notebook, but he refrained. Instead he sat and thought. *Georgie Mackie, why is she dead?*

Why would you write slut when nobody seems to say she is? There's not a strong enough suggestion to back it up. She would be leading a heck of a double life. And as a headmistress, school is so focused on itself, so many people, it would be hard to conduct an affair, not without rumours flying. And there didn't seem to be rumours that stuck when it came to sleeping around.

Yes, she was progressive, yes. She'd even gone lying face down, bikini top off in her garden, invoking the wrath of Pauline Drummond. But had it caused somebody to kill her? Why, it was her own garden. It wasn't like she'd popped round to somebody's house and sunbathed there. She had every right to do what she wanted in her own garden. And she hadn't been explicit in any way.

Macleod rubbed his face. It was getting harder these days. You came away, and you just kept on the go. The old brain, mind, the body, it didn't work for so long anymore. He'd thought when he'd stepped up to DCI that he was basically handing Hope what she needed. And then he thought he'd missed it and he would need to get back in the game for a bit, whatever way he could. But things had changed.

The Forseti group had taken a bigger toll on him than he'd ever thought. But also now, he was covering. He wasn't buzzing. Not this time. Oh yes, he'd do the job. He'd get to the bottom of it. That, after all, was what he was. But he was aching. It would be nice to wake up, roll over and just hold on to Jane for an hour. It would be perfect not to be stuck away in hotel, or even school accommodation, with Jane up the road.

Macleod was getting to an age when he realised that the time ahead could be a lot less than the time behind. Jane had moved in to be with him. But if he hung on for another five years plus or whatever, what was the guarantee that Jane would still be there? He didn't think she would leave him. But sometimes these things were taken out of your hands. The good Lord could call you home whenever he wanted. But he called more people later in life than he did in the earlier stages. And the later stages of life were what Macleod was getting to.

The toll had also been taken on the body. His knees hurt. Sometimes shoulders would just randomly start feeling sore. The eyesight wasn't as good as it used to be either. And sometimes he just wasn't quick enough. Not to how he used to be. Not to the way he handled things.

He sighed. Again, he started to think. What was he dealing with here? Something under his skin was saying this was not some sort of love triangle. This was not some prude on hell-bent vengeance against those who had sullied their school. Something else was at work. He could feel it. But then again, he couldn't say what. And that's what was truly bothering him.

Chapter 13

Macleod spent about an hour and a half just sitting on the bench in the middle of the school grounds. He thought about how he had told Ross to get out and do some legwork. But this was how he thought. This is where the brain got into gear. This is where Macleod came into his own as a detective. He could see things. He could make them match when other people couldn't.

There would have been no point in Hope sitting like this. She wouldn't have got anywhere. Even Perry wouldn't have worked this way. Perry needed to be out and about. Things occurred to Perry as he bumbled around. Not so with Macleod.

He had his moments. When he ran the murder squad in what was Hope's current position, he had his office and he had stared out of that window so many times for so long. If they said to him, where did you solve your murders? He would say there. That's where the real thinking was done. His new office had a rubbish window. So maybe it was a good thing he was here. Able to get out and about. Able to breathe in the fresh air of the west coast as he dealt with this horror.

'Inspector! Inspector!'

No, thought Macleod. *It's that Fotheringham-Smythe woman.*

What does she want now?

'Inspector! Inspector!' Macleod stood up and turned to face the deputy headmistress.

'Have you seen James Kershaw?'

'Well, good afternoon to you. No, I haven't,' said Macleod.

'Well, we were having a staff meeting. He's meant to be in the meeting. It's a senior staff meeting. We're all there, and James didn't turn up.'

'Well, I was speaking to him this morning. I interviewed him. Why do you ask me? Couldn't you get some of the rest of the school to run around and find him?'

'I've been to his office. He's not there. In the gymnasium hall, he's not there. We've been everywhere.'

'What about the classes he had this morning?'

'I've asked them. He was there for every one.'

'I saw him with his netball group,' said Macleod.

'And then he was in the gym, supervising the oldest group.'

Macleod wondered what supervise meant in practice but the man was missing, and this could be a problem.

'Have you called him? Have you tried his mobile?'

'Do I look like a buffoon, Inspector? Of course, I've tried his mobile. It's ringing out.'

'Has anybody heard it go off?'

'No. But it is ringing out. James's is usually on silent, anyway. It will vibrate.'

'So, he's not answering anything. Have you gone through all the social media? WhatsApp, Messenger, all that to contact him? See if anybody can reach him?'

'We've done it all. We've left a message, as you can see. Look,' said the deputy headmistress, handing over her phone, pointing Macleod to the messages sent. 'He's answering nothing. Can you help?'

Macleod stopped for a moment and thought. *What was the best action?*

'Yes, I can,' he said. He picked up the phone and dialled for Susan.

'It's Susan.'

'Where are you?' asked Macleod.

'Down in Applecross. Just coming back.'

'Fine, I'll talk to you when you're here. Perry with you?'

'Yes.' Macleod closed down the call and rang Ross.

'Sir?'

'Ross, James Kershaw is missing. You need to round up uniform. Get a search party going across the grounds. See if he's here.'

'Susan can do that. I'll give her a call.'

'Susan's on her way back. She can take over, but get it up and get it going, please, Ross.'

'Yes, sir,' said Ross, but Macleod could hear the annoyance in his voice.

'Mrs Fotheringham-Smythe, what we'll do is we'll get the police constables we have to search. I suggest you do nothing else with the rest of the school. Keep it running and keep it normal. Okay? I want your senior staff, if they're meant to be in a meeting, to check anywhere staff can go. Just in case he's off seeing Donnie for any reason or whatever. See if he's left the grounds.'

'He won't have left the grounds. We note out when we leave the grounds.'

'I appreciate that,' said Macleod, 'but if you haven't realised, I'm here for a reason. There's been a murder. People don't always follow the rules when there's a murder. You're generally trying to get away with things. So, if you could get the staff to check the staff areas for me, please. I'll get the constables searching the rest of the school. Including those outbuildings over there.'

'The empty ones.'

'Yes, deputy headmistress, the empty ones.'

'They won't find anything there. They're just empty. Everything got cleared out.'

'Why did it get cleared out?' asked Macleod.

'Asbestos. Anyway, are we going to find him?'

'We're going to do our best,' said Macleod.

He turned and started heading towards the uniformed sergeant and was delighted to find Ross had beaten him. They didn't have many men on site. Eight. They still needed a couple on the cordon, preventing the press getting any closer. Macleod had insisted that all press stay outside the grounds of the school. School was still running despite this.

However, Macleod knew that such a deployment of uniform within the grounds would be spotted by the press at some point. Soon be on to him asking what was going on. Sometimes he wished they would just clear off. The press often got in the way. Yes, true, sometimes they could be helpful, but that was despite themselves, not because of them.

Macleod went to the staff room, which was where the meeting was to take place. One by one, the other teachers left as classes were still running, but this was the hub. From here, they would search on the basis James would have been making his way there. Macleod thought it best if he manned the central position. Beside him was a uniformed sergeant while Ross was taking on some of the legwork that Macleod had asked for by searching some of the other areas.

'We're not finding anything. It's a pretty difficult place to get lost in,' said the uniformed sergeant. 'The trouble is that if he has gone missing, he will not be in the populated areas, and there aren't that many other areas.'

'What about the buildings that got emptied?'

'Well, we searched those first, and he's not there. We're going around the grounds too. They're extensive but not that easy to hide somebody in. We searched the dormitories, and I started calling the young women back, so we could look in and around their stuff too.'

'I bet the deputy headmistress wasn't happy about that,' said Macleod.

'She wanted it all hushed up. When you'd given her the shove-off,' said the sergeant, 'she came at me. Oh, we need to do this, we need to do that, we can't have it disrupting the school, we can't have the young women being informed that he's missing. Panic and dread and all the rest of it.'

'She has got a point,' said Macleod, 'but we need to find him.'

Macleod stood waiting and looked out the window where he saw the deputy headmistress. In the distance, there appeared to be one of the girls running towards her. She was dressed in shorts and a t-shirt, running wildly, desperately screaming.

Macleod bolted from the staff room through the corridor and out the door at the side to see Mrs Fotheringham-Smythe cuddling the girl, telling her it would be all right.

'What's up?' asked Macleod.

'Girls changing by the gymnasium.'

Macleod didn't wait for an explanation, but turned and ran. It was further than he remembered, and he was running out of puff by the time he got to the gymnasium. He burst in, having seen it earlier that morning, and remembered that the

105

girls changing was a little down from the shower area that was employed by Kershaw. However, there was a large batch of screaming girls around the area. Some of the uniformed police officers had arrived and were trying to get the girls to step back.

'Inspector coming through,' shouted Macleod. 'Everyone, back. Constable, get them out of here. Take them into the sports hall, somewhere; just get them away from this area.'

Macleod bumped into a girl who was weeping. She grabbed hold of Macleod, holding him tight, burying her face in his stomach, bitterly crying her eyes out. Macleod took hold of her shoulders.

'Go with the constable,' he said. 'You need to go with the constable. I have to work.'

He almost peeled her off him before a constable put an arm to her, asking her to accompany him. The gathered throng, however, even as she was escorted away, formed a small semicircle around the entrance to the girls' changing area. Macleod stepped cautiously forward ahead of them.

He turned left through a door and then through another door and then was in the changing area. As Macleod stepped in, he called out 'Police,' but there was no answer. Stepping further in, he saw rows of clothes, school uniforms, hanging up on pegs. It was where the girls got changed, after all, and there seemed to have been a frenzy in leaving for the clothes were in a state, here, there and wherever. But there was no other strangeness in the changing room.

Macleod walked forward to the end of it. There were showers around the corner. And he stopped for a moment.

'This is Detective Inspector Macleod. Is there anyone within the shower area? Is there anyone in there? I'm going to have to come in and search it. However, if someone is in there in an indecent state, please advise me.'

Macleod waited, but there was nothing. Slowly he walked forward, turned the corner at the edge of what was a communal shower. He thought that was unusual. After all, weren't female showers individual? Wasn't that the thing? It wasn't like men, who were used to a communal shower.

When he turned the corner, however, all thoughts of the appropriateness or not of the showering area vanished in an instant. On the floor was a female mannequin, like the ones you occasionally saw in shop windows prior to being dressed. However, this one was pinned to the ground. Straddling the mannequin was James Kershaw. He was utterly naked. Beyond him on the wall was the word 'traitor.'

Macleod stepped forward quickly. He checked for a pulse in different areas. He checked for breath. There was nothing. Absolutely nothing. Macleod looked at his watch. He left the man not that long ago. He could only have been dead for a while. Five hours? Six at the most?

Macleod reached to James Kershaw's arms. Previously, Georgie Mackie had been set in place when she died, and the rigor mortis in her arms had kept her in the provocative sexual position she'd died in. *Surely this couldn't have been enough time*, thought Macleod. *Five or six hours? Could you have been sure? Could you have . . .*

He reached forward, and touched one of James's arms. It was then he realised it was tied. The arms were behind James's head, but they had a clear wire wrapped around the wrists that were holding them to his neck.

Macleod knelt down and realised that the feet and the knees were also pinned around under the mannequin. He was held in this position by restraint, unlike Georgie Mackie. Macleod took a step back.

'Traitor.' Someone thought he was a traitor. James Kershaw. What had he done? Had he or Georgie been having an affair with somebody else? James wasn't having an affair with anyone, was he? Had James betrayed someone sexually?

Many conclusions jumped into Macleod's mind. He didn't find it difficult to see James Kershaw putting it about, as they would say at the station. Maybe somebody else was pregnant. *Was it the girl in town, Keira Saunders? Had Georgie Mackie ended up sexually active with him. Was there someone else he was at it with?*

The man clearly had an appetite that wasn't satisfied. Macleod had watched him looking at those girls that morning, and he knew something was up with the man. Now, if he was simply having sex with lots of legal if young, girls, that was okay, at least in the eyes of the law. If it was consensual, there was nothing for the law to bring against him. However, that didn't stop others from making their own law. There was a cough from behind Macleod, and Perry walked up beside him.

'Another one,' said Perry. 'And in daytime, how on earth?'

How on earth indeed? thought Macleod.

Chapter 14

Macleod watched Jona Nakamura moving back and forward across the scene. Of all her colleagues, she was the smallest, a diminutive Asian woman. What she lacked in height, she made up for with savvy and enthusiasm. Macleod was always impressed by how her forensic team looked to her. Yes, they would get on with their own work, but she was the first port of call. The entire operation was so smooth.

Jona was a calming influence on an investigation. Even when you stepped out of line, tried to enter a scene with the wrong gear on, or were about to contaminate something, she never got angry. Instead, Jona was quick to act. She could be brusque with you, letting you know without shouting at you that you'd made an error, and she wasn't impressed. On the other hand, if you were struggling, Jona was a great source of help.

Right now, Macleod was waiting on a report from her, and she'd seen him several times waiting on the edge of the cordon. He knew that whatever pressure she was under, she wouldn't relent, doing her job until she was ready for him to enter the scene with her. Only then would she give her report. Macleod appreciated that professionalism, but it didn't make him any less agitated as he waited to hear what she would say.

It looked like a repeat killing, and the trouble with repeat killings, as Macleod always said, was it wasn't the first-time repeat. It was the second, the third and the continuation that meant you had to act quickly. You had to get to the killer. A single murder and you didn't know if there was another coming. Two, that usually meant there was more on the way.

Perry and Susan were organising the uniform detail around the school. More were arriving with the expected increased media attention now that there was a second killing. The school had almost got back to normal after the first, but Macleod knew that this would shake things up completely. Whereas before, the deputy headmistress might have been able to phone parents and say, 'Look, it's okay. This has happened; we're dealing with it; it's unexpected.' With a double killer on the loose, no parent was going to want their children to still be there, and the press would come in droves.

One murder was juicy, especially with the way the head-mistress had been found, but most of that had been kept quiet. Therefore it was just the death of a headmistress. With the second death though, questions would be asked, and the press always get out any juicy details. It would sell papers. The positions the two victims were found in, the words with them would sell papers all right.

Macleod could see it, how their sex lives—fact or fiction— would be plastered over the press. Not in graphic detail though, because these were papers after all. Instead with a salacious-ness and possible inuendo that was totally inappropriate for two people having died. Macleod didn't read papers; he hated them with an extreme passion. The only time he ever went into them was when he had to, because it was related to the case, because he was looking for something within them.

Normally, he didn't even clock the news. Misinformation could skew your mind. As a detective, it had to be clear; it had to be focused only on what was in front of him; otherwise, flights of fancy came in, and you ended up missing the blindingly obvious.

There was a wave from Jona, and Macleod turned, found a suit, and put the coverall on in the nearby changing room. When he came back, Jona was waiting.

'Sorry, Seoras,' she said. 'It took a wee bit longer than I thought. I just wanted to check a few things.'

'You're doing your job. It's fine,' said Macleod. 'What have you got for me?'

'Well, similar to our first victim. I've found needle marks, and I think James has been injected with some sort of muscle relaxant. Something to make him pliable, but immobile.'

'Do you have any rope marks?'

'Similar,' said Jona. 'But again, there's not much here to tie to. That's the thing. I actually think things were brought in for him to be tied to.'

'And he's died in that position.'

'Yes, and he's been placed so at his centre of gravity means he doesn't topple over. It's almost a macabre work of art,' said Jona. There was no laughter in her comment. Instead, her eyes looked deep and seriously at Macleod. 'You have to have a complete disrespect of people for this. I understand it, but I don't want to.'

'Well, have you ever overstepped your mark? Tell me what you're thinking,' said Macleod.

'It's one thing, isn't it, Seoras, to actually kill someone? But people do that in a fit of rage. People do that out of anger.

But to actually position them like this, to actually manipulate their body, or about-to-die body, that requires a coldness. This is a crime of passion, we're led to believe. Traitor. But you don't paint traitor up after casually holding this guy together, manipulating his body so that he doesn't topple over. I mean, if it was a crime of passion, you would just kill him. And then . . .'

'But they're making a statement.'

'What statement?' said Jona 'With our first victim, the statement was on the wall, "Slut." People know what that is. You don't have to put on a graphic demonstration. This one here, traitor, another graphic demonstration. I'm not buying it. The other thing is that I'm not sure we're going to find anything. It all looks to have been swept, it's been cleared. It's really well done.'

'You say really well done. There are plenty of professionals who go around cleaning guns and stuff after shooting people, causing murder.'

'No, above that. Above that, Seoras. This is my level. I'm not sure I could clean this up better.'

'You said that as well, didn't you, with our first victim?'

'I think whoever's involved in this knows how to clean things up. Again, it's not a crime of passion. It doesn't sit with me.'

'I see where you're coming from,' said Macleod. 'However, we are talking teachers here. We're talking people with method. People who are used to making plans. So, maybe.'

'You're the detective,' said Jona. 'I said it's not my place. I'm just . . .'

'No, no, no,' said Macleod. 'Thank you. You find out any more, let me know.'

'Oh, and they were rushed this time. His arms are held by

wire, not by rigour mortis. They had to rush and didn't have the same amount of time.'

'Thank you,' said Macleod.

Macleod turned and saw Perry at the edge of the cordon walking carefully over. He pulled down his hood but was intercepted by the deputy headmistress before he could reach Perry.

'I've had people calling,' said Miss Fotheringham-Smythe. 'Parents. Parents looking to take their children away. It's out already. It's out. Parents asking me if there's a sex ring going on within the school, people asking me . . .'

Macleod put his hand up. 'It's a second murder,' he said. 'You can expect it will get out. You've got three hundred girls here and you're telling me none of them are going to speak out? Victims have been seen. I'm amazed frankly,' said Macleod, 'that it hasn't got more press coverage and wider spread than it has.'

'I don't care, Inspector,' said the deputy headmistress. 'Frankly, I think you need to be keeping it quiet. You need to be—'

Macleod put his hand up. 'My job is to find out who's doing this. There will be a police cordon maintained around the grounds. The press will be kept at a distance, but they will come. You live in a free country, and they are entitled to come and ask questions. I don't like it. I frankly could do with them getting off my back when I do my job, but that's the way our country works. You don't like that? Talk to the Prime Minister. Talk to your MP. Don't come talking to me. I need to deal with this. You need to deal with those parents.'

Perry was now hovering over Macleod's shoulder and Macleod turned slightly before looking back and giving the

Deputy Headmistress a stare that said, I need to talk to my Constable. The woman tutted and walked off, and Macleod thought he saw a faint smile on Perry's lips.

'What is it, Perry?' asked Macleod.

'Press are here in big numbers. We've got them contained to outside the school grounds. I've told the uniform lads to watch for anyone trying to jump over the walls or sneak in by other routes.'

'At least this is contained inside. As long as nobody gets in here, the story's only on second hand report. We don't want any photographs. We don't want anything like that.'

'Uniform are doing okay. They've shipped a few more in from Glasgow with the extra attention we're now going to get. Jona say much?'

'Same as last time. Immobilized. Balanced. Killed. And left. Bit of extra wire this time. But she made a good point. The words that were written up. When you put up the word slut, why do you need to make a statement to show it with the person? You could just leave them naked. Why? Why this mannequin? Why this sexual position? Jona was getting at it being overplayed.'

'She's got a point,' said Perry.

'Jona also said that it's spotless. She's not confident she's going to pick up any other evidence. Feels the scene was handled by someone of her level. Her understanding.'

'Okay,' said Perry. 'From my reading of the files, Lily Walters was a forensic officer for a time, wasn't she?'

'Yes,' said Macleod. 'Which is interesting, of course. It could be used to frame her. Maybe that's why all this trouble has been gone to, to put the blame on her.'

'But then you'd have to get somebody in who knew how to

do this.'

Macleod stopped. He was going round and round here with this. He needed to cut back.

'They're also wanting a statement, the press,' said Perry. 'What should I tell them?'

'Just a moment,' said Macleod. He looked around him and saw Ross talking to some uniformed officers. He waved them over.

'Yes, sir,' said Ross.

'Ross, I want you to do the press statement. I need to talk to the members of staff. They were in a meeting together. I need to see what was going on.'

'Press statement. You want me to do the press statement?'

'It's not a problem, is it?'

'That's Hope's domain really. She's always good with the press. Female angle always worked.'

'And no doubt our higher masters would say it's good having a gay man doing it as well,' said Macleod. He instantly regretted that. It was tetchy. He was snappy.

'I can do it if you want,' said Ross.

'Sorry,' said Macleod. 'I want you to do it because I need to go. You're more than capable. You'll be fine. Forget what I just said.'

'No,' said Ross, 'you're probably right, they would enjoy that and think it's great, but like Hope, I wouldn't want to be used as some sort of token figure.'

'And you never will be with me,' said Macleod. 'I want you to do this because I don't want to do it. I need to do something else.'

'Yes, sir. I'll get on that.'

He was about to walk away when he thought of something,

115

and he turned and shouted across the gruesome scene towards Jona. She came walking over, put her hand on her hip. 'You didn't have enough time with me?'

'Just thought of something. This mobilisation,' said Macleod. 'How long's it last?'

'What do you mean?'

'When would it wear off?'

'They were dead by the time it wore off,' said Jona. 'That's how it would work. You would immobilise them, replace them, then you kill them, and then rigor mortis sets in, and then they're stuck in that position.'

'No, no, no,' said Macleod. 'From the moment you immobilise them, how long have you got to get them into that position?'

'It depends on the dosage. You could repeat the injection an hour or two later. Keep them in that state if needed; it wouldn't be difficult. The difficult bit, or certainly the awkward bit, is then getting them into that position. Holding them in that position, and then once you kill them, keeping them there until rigor mortis is strong enough that they are fixed, so to speak. With this one, they needed an extra bit of wire. It's a finely balanced thing as well. There's a calculation to be made there. You get the centre of gravity in the right place.'

Macleod nodded and turned. Once again, the deputy headmistress was on the warpath for him. He'd just sent her away, and she was coming back. But fortunately, he needed to ask her something now.

'Inspector, I really must have a word. Have you seen the amount of press at the front gate?'

'No, but I'm in no doubt it will be large,' said Macleod. 'Don't worry about it. Detective Sergeant Ross is dealing with them.

James today. What was his schedule like? How long were you working this morning? I know I went to see him.'

'Well, he had . . .' She stopped for a moment and thought. 'He had a couple of classes.'

'Yes, I know I saw him take some of the girls for class.'

'But then he was off for at least one before he was meant to come for the meeting. And then at the meeting there, we were a good half hour plus. More than that, actually. He would have had maybe three hours of being unseen, thinking about it.'

'Could you round up your senior staff? I need to talk to you again.'

'Well, as long as you get on with the press. Push them back. Tell them to stay in Applecross. This is a school. We can't have people peering in. I've already had parents asking for girls to go home. I'm having to arrange that. Do you realise how damaging this is for the school?'

'Do you realise how damaging it's been for James and Georgie?' said Macleod.

'I can't do anything about them, can I? But I have a duty to the school and a duty to maintain its reputation. And the tabloid press and whoever else out there are going to ruin it.'

'Well, I'm afraid I can't do anything about that. The school will just have to ride what bad press comes its way,' said Macleod. 'I, however, have an investigation to run and I would like to see your senior staff. Please gather them. Advise me when they're there.'

Macleod turned away and walked out of the building to get some air. As he stepped outside, he was approached by two schoolgirls.

'He's dead,' said one girl. There were tears in her eyes.

'I'm afraid so,' said Macleod.

'Were they at it together?' asked the other girl.

'I'm sorry?' said Macleod.

'The headmistress and James, were they lovers? Did she have somebody else?'

'I can't answer that,' said Macleod. 'Even if I could, I wouldn't. There's a time and a proper place, and at the moment I have two victims. And I think the best thing to do is not to engage in wild speculation,' said Macleod.

'But they left her. They said she was a slut.'

'I'm sorry?' said Macleod. 'I can't.'

The girl tilted forward. She was crying fully now, and she'd landed on Macleod's shoulder. She was tall, maybe close to eighteen. Part of Macleod felt that grandfatherly instinct. She was in pain. He wanted to give her just a cuddle. Nothing strange in that, but to even think about doing that, to even enact that in any way, the rumours would be everywhere. Instead, he took two hands, gently tilted the girl back off him, and then turned to her friend.

'Maybe you should take care of her, yeah? Give her a hug or something. Just take her somewhere and let her cry for a bit.'

The girl's friend nodded, turned and walked off, consoling her friend.

Of all the cases, Hope. Why aren't you here? A girl's school and the detective is an older white man. Press will have a field day with this one. And guess what? There's a sexual motive involved too.

He'd phoned Jane the night before because she was fairly grounded and he could talk to her about things like this. He'd told her how uncomfortable he was. She'd been positive. Told him he'd be fine. Told him he was a professional. But she also reminded him, stay aloof. It's the best way because emotions would run high. *Emotions always ran high in a murder case,*

Macleod thought. He sighed. Macleod needed to sort this out quickly and get out of here. He needed to get the senior staff together.

Chapter 15

What position was she in? Was he in the same position? Did it look authentic?'

Perry stared at the journalist. 'What paper are you from?' asked Perry.

'I'm from Libido Holdings.'

Libido Holdings, thought Perry. *Libido Holdings is—*'

'You're from a smut magazine.'

'Adult entertainment magazine,' corrected the journalist.

'I'm dealing with a murder here.'

'Juicy murder though. Apparently, she was quite a looker.'

'Get him out of here,' said Perry to a constable.

'He's at the edge of the cordon. On what grounds?'

'Is that your car over there?' asked Perry to the journalist.

'No, mine's parked over there.'

'That's illegally parked. Ticket him, get him moved,' said Perry. The uniformed constable gave Perry a nod and engaged with the journalist, asking him to come with him and telling him to move the car.

Perry was assaulted with more questions, this time from more reputable papers. Although the questions were reasonable, Perry wouldn't be answering any of them.

'There'll be a statement coming shortly. We'll advise you as and when,' said Perry.

'Detective Constable,' came a voice from behind Perry. He turned and a uniformed female constable was standing beside Iris Adams. 'Lady said she'd like a word with you, if that's okay.'

'Of course,' said Perry, 'thank you.' He walked towards Iris Adams and then pointed, taking her to a distance well inside the cordon and behind a building so they couldn't be seen.

'Not a place for us to discuss anything out there. They're like wolves, hungry for anything.'

'I've got something to tell you,' said Iris. 'I wonder if you'd want to come to my flat.'

'Come to your flat? You can tell me here,' said Perry.

'No,' said Iris. 'It's a bit delicate. I need to tell you in the flat. I need to show you something.'

'Just a moment,' said Perry. He turned, stepped back round from the building and looked. Susan was up near the cordon as well. He waved his hand, and she came over. He spun back to Iris. 'I've got Detective Cunningham coming over. She can go with you. You're able to tell her anything you can tell me.'

'No, I want you to come,' said Iris.

'You want me to come? Why me?'

'It's difficult. I think you'll be easier to talk to.'

'Wait a moment,' said Perry. He turned and intercepted Susan before she reached the building. They were now about twenty feet away from Iris, and in a hushed tone, Perry said to Susan, 'Iris wants me to go. She says she's got information, wants me to go round to her flat, wants to talk to me.'

'I can go,' said Susan.

'That's why I called you over. I thought that would make

sense, but when I said to her you were coming, she said she wanted to talk to me, specifically me. It's strange, isn't it?'

'Very. Why don't I join you?'

'I don't think she's going to go for that,' said Perry. 'Said she's got to show me something.'

Susan glared at Perry. 'Given what's been going on here recently, are you sure that's wise?'

'What, you think she's going to seduce me?' Perry stopped. Given their recent history, it might not have been the best thing to say in front of Susan.

'That's been known,' she said, almost regretfully.

'I'm a big boy. I think I can handle it, but if I'm not back, and I haven't contacted you in twenty minutes, call me.'

'You sure?'

'Yes,' said Perry. 'I think something's up here. I was talking to Macleod about it. Something doesn't feel right.'

'We've had two people murdered and left starkers with mannequins in school buildings. Which bit about this do you think isn't right?' asked Susan.

'True,' said Perry. 'But just a feeling. Macleod's got it too, I think.'

'Well, if the boys have got a feeling, then I guess us girls better let you get on with it.'

'Okay, but make sure you ring me in twenty minutes if I haven't come back to you.'

'Will do. Take care,' said Susan.

Susan turned back to the cordon, and Perry went back to Lily. She showed him round to the little flat she had, one of the accommodation buildings for the staff. She opened the front door and invited him in. It was small. There was a living room, what Perry presumed was the bedroom at the rear, a kitchen off to one side, and a bathroom. Iris pointed into the living room.

'Sit down, I'll make a cup of tea,' she said.

'Well, you can just talk to me now,' said Perry, still standing in the hall.

'No, no, take a seat. Do you want something stronger than tea? I can get you something stronger. There's decent wine in here I could offer.'

Iris Adams had seemed shy when the team had first met her, and now Perry was slightly confused. She was a good-looking young woman. Long red hair tied up, but Perry noticed it was braided today, not in a ponytail. Her figure was trim, and she wore a blouse that emphasized her figure. She played the slightly shy-looking woman, and yet she was the one who invited him in.

Why? thought Perry. He had Tanya now and was more than happy in himself and with their relationship. Iris wasn't a threat to that which is why he'd come on his own. Perry was more interested in why suddenly one of the teachers wanted him to come with her.

'What is it you want to tell me?' asked Perry, as Iris came back in with tea. She handed him a cup, which already had the tea in it, and asked if he wanted milk. Perry didn't want the tea, but he shook his head and dutifully took a sip to show appreciation.

Iris put her hand up to her chest, as if protecting herself.

'I think Donnie is worth watching.'

'Why are you saying that?' asked Perry.

'I don't like to say,' she said, but she gave a shiver. 'I hope you don't think this arrogant of me, but I think he . . . well, I think he has a peephole in my flat.'

'Sorry?' blurted Perry.

'A peephole. I think he's watching me.'

'What makes you think that?' asked Perry.

'I was having a bath. In fact, several times when I've had a bath, I . . . well . . . I climb in and I lie there. I just had a feeling of being watched. It was quiet, and I thought I could hear movement. Then I thought nothing of it. I thought I heard a noise. Scratching.'

'While you were in the bath,' said Perry.

'Washing myself. Sometimes I use oils in the bath. I like to soak. Like to have candles. It's a very private thing,' she said. 'It's a time when you . . . well . . . And then I thought someone was watching. I just had that feeling.'

'Okay,' said Perry. 'So you think you're being watched while in the bath?'

'Come with me,' said Iris. She took Perry and showed him the bathroom. It was small, and there were several candles, unlit currently, around the bath.

'This is a flat,' said Perry, 'but you're on the bottom floor. So you'd have to be in the flat above to see down? Or is he looking in through the window?'

There was a small window in the bathroom, but it was up high and Perry couldn't see how you would get at an angle to look in. Besides that, it was frosted, a bathroom window to stop people seeing anything.

'My bathroom isn't underneath the other flat. There's a flat roof above it.'

'And you think he's looking in?'

'There,' she said, pointing at the ceiling. 'I would be here, totally exposed, washing myself, bathing, and he'd be watching.'

The woman seemed to shudder, but Perry decided the facts needed to be looked at, and so he peered up to the ceiling. *Was there something there?* The ceiling was pockmarked here and there, for it was not in great repair.

'You wouldn't have a small pair of stepladders or even a chair?'

'Of course, Inspector,' said Iris.

'It's just Constable,' said Perry almost absentmindedly. The woman brushed past him, her hand lingering on him. Perry wondered what on earth she was doing.

She came back with a chair, and Perry stood on it, looking up at the ceiling. There were several holes. But there was one he could put his hand up to and put a finger deep into it. It touched something at the other end.

'That feels odd,' he said, 'but I can't see through it. I can't see anywhere up here on the ceiling where anyone could look down.'

'I've heard him. The breathing. Like a hungry animal.'

'Just a moment,' said Perry. He left the bathroom, walked out the front door of the flat, and tried to locate where the bathroom would be from the outside. He could see it, and there was an escape ladder from the flat above. Perry used that to get onto the flat roof, which the bathroom would be under. He ran his hands across the roof and eventually found a little black piece of rubber. It was hard to see located within the black tar that covered the roof, but Perry pulled at it and it came away. He looked down into the gap that was left behind and thought he could see the bathroom.

He was about to shout and tell Iris to lie in the bath so he could look down upon her. Then he could see just how much of a view would come from this position. But then he thought of Susan's words and instead picked up his phone to call her. Susan Cunningham arrived on the flat roof shortly after.

'The flat's got a peephole. I'm going to go back inside and lie in the bath, and I want you to tell me, when I come out, how much you can see.'

'Okay,' said Susan. 'But tell me, how did the rain not come in?'

'She said she thinks she's been being watched while in the bath. When I got up here, there was a little rubber piece that was blocking any ingress through that hole. Take it out, and you have a view into the bath. I was going to get her to sit in the bath so I could see, but she's acting strangely. Very familiar. Almost as if . . .'

'What?' asked Susan.

'Almost like she's trying to attract me or play me. I don't want to burst that bubble. So, I'm going to go inside into the bath. You can tell me what you can see. Don't tell her anything. Don't shout to me. I'll just lie in the bath and pretend I'm looking up at the hole to see what I can see.'

'Okay,' said Susan.

'Can you also breathe deeply?' said Perry.

'Breathe deeply?'

'Yes. Like a man who's, well . . . you know, enjoying himself while he watches.'

Susan stared at him. 'Really?'

'That's what she said. I want to know if I can hear the breathing.'

Perry went back to the ladder. He realised that this roof was reasonably well hidden. You'd have to come round through the alcove at the back of the buildings to get to the ladder and then get up there. Re-entering the flat, Iris followed him through to the bathroom as Perry jumped in and looked up.

'I think you're right, Iris,' he said. 'You've definitely got a peephole up there. Nothing up there to say that it's Donnie, though.'

'He looks at us all, though. The women. Doesn't have anyone. Doesn't say much. That sort of person, isn't he?'

'I really wouldn't know,' said Perry. On the other hand, Perry would talk to him, but the man seemed simple and not like that at all. Perry sat back, looking up, and the hole to the outside showed sky and then showed what he thought must have been an eye. He closed his eyes and listened. He could hear Susan breathing. Perry stood up, climbed out of the bath and turned to Iris.

'I'm going to get the forensics to come and look at this. I'm also going to see if any of your colleagues have anything similar.'

There was a knock at the flat door. When Iris opened it, Perry could see Mrs Fotheringham-Smythe standing on the other side of the door.

'The detective inspector's looking for you. Wants us all to gather. Oh, Constable.'

'The Constable's just helping me with something,' said Iris, again lifting her hand up to touch the nape of her neck in what Perry considered to be a rather strange reaction.

'On your own in the flat?' said a shocked looking Mrs Fotheringham-Smythe.

'No, he's not. I'm here with him. We were just checking out some peepholes,' said Susan. Mrs Fotheringham-Smythe turned, almost looking annoyed at Susan, before turning back towards Iris.

'Well, come along.'

'We'll come too,' said Perry. 'I need to talk to my inspector. I think we're going to have to have a look at everyone's dwellings.'

'I'm sure it's Donnie,' said Iris, making her way past Miss Fotheringham-Smythe. 'He has those eyes.'

Perry followed the women towards the staff room. In his head, something wasn't right. *Donnie didn't have those eyes. Donnie was innocent*, Perry thought. *Maybe he could do with another assessment. He'd ask Macleod.*

Chapter 16

Perry arrived at the staff room to find his boss awaiting the senior staff. Most were already there, and Perry asked Macleod to step outside of the room so Susan and he could talk to him.

'What's up, Perry?' asked Macleod.

'I was approached by Iris Adams, and to cut a long story short, I went to her flat where she said that she felt she was being watched while in the bathroom. We've discovered that there is a peephole to that bathroom from the flat roof above. It was covered up with a piece of rubber so that the outside rain and elements couldn't be let in unless it was being used. It's a neat-looking job, and it's definitely positioned so that, well . . . you could see everything while someone was in the bath. Iris is blaming Donnie. She says she could hear breathing from outside. I got Susan to stay on the roof while I was in the bath, and I could hear her breathing.'

'Okay,' said Macleod. 'What would you need to put a peephole in there? If you cut in, wouldn't you make a mess?'

'Well, yes,' said Perry. 'I guess you would.'

'But what about Donnie?' asked Susan. 'I know Perry doesn't think it's anything to do with him, but Donnie is the janitor.

Donnie would have tools. I assumed Donnie would be able to get into people's flats without them being there even, if there was work to do.'

'Just a moment,' said Macleod. He opened the door to the staff room, looked in and called over the deputy headmistress. Mrs Fotheringham-Smythe stepped outside of the room, and Macleod asked her to close the door.

'Can you tell me who has access to your private quarters? Not just yours, but to all the senior staff.'

'Well, I'm not sure anyone does. Well, technically I would, I guess. There is a set of keys which are locked away. But no one has access to those, and you have to sign for them.'

'And who signs those out?'

'Well, the staff will have their own keys, so they've no need for their own flats. If I want to go into somebody else's room, I would normally ask. Also, Donnie has access to it, but he asks and signs in the book to say when he's been in.'

'Is it common for Donnie to be in other people's houses?'

'Well, throughout a year, yes, because there's work to do. Donnie's the janitor, so if you've got any issues, he'll be in. If he's checking the radiators or anything like that, he'll be there. He bleeds them occasionally. Yes, Donnie would have been in and out in the course of a year, through just about everyone's accommodation. It's perfectly normal. He signs in and out.'

'And he would do this while people weren't in.'

'Yes.'

'Thank you,' said Macleod. Mrs Frotheringham-Smythe gave him a look and then returned to the staff room. Once she'd gone in, Macleod turned back to his colleagues.

'Well, Donnie has access. And access that is not overseen.'

'But Mrs Frotheringham-Smythe has a key. And there are

keys you can get access to,' said Perry. 'What's to stop someone not signing the book?'

'Indeed,' said Macleod. 'I think you should check the other rooms,' said Macleod. 'The senior staff are just gathering. I'll announce it to them.'

As he went to open the door, Pauline Drummond arrived, dressed in a rather baggy jumper and a long skirt. She was maintaining her rather more demure dress sense compared to the rest of the younger staff. Her hair was tied up once again, and as she approached, she turned to Macleod.

'Another one. This is the problem with sex. This is the problem when it's thrown in people's faces. This is how people react. This has come from Georgie's . . .'

'Can I stop you there?' said Macleod. 'If you step inside the room, I have an announcement to make to everyone.'

Pauline Drummond looked at him with fury, annoyed at being cut off. But she obliged and entered the room. Macleod followed and asked the staff to sit down.

'We have found a peephole in Iris's flat,' said Macleod. 'I wish to search the other flats to see if there are any others. Would I have the permission of everyone to use the keys that are held here and check your flats? We'll not be rummaging through your stuff. It's merely to see if there are any peepholes.'

Mrs Fotheringham-Smythe stood up. 'Well, I don't see why not. Seems perfectly reasonable. I'll get you the key. Or rather, the keys.'

She left, and Macleod waited for objections from others, but there were none. Not even a hint. He found that strange. But when Mrs Fotheringham-Smythe came back, he took the keys and handed them to Perry and Susan.

'Take one of Jona's crew with you. They would have a better

131

idea about what tools might be used.'

'I think I can manage that,' said Perry. But regardless, when they departed the room, Susan and he sought Jona. She said her people were busy, but if they found something, they were to mark it and she would send someone round to look. If these holes were made a long time ago, she doubted there'd be any evidence left worth picking up, but she would send somebody round afterwards to see.

Perry and Susan started at James Kershaw's flat. Most of the flats were of a similar size, and it took them a while before Perry saw a hole in the living room. The living room had its own roof, which was unusual among the flats. On the outside, by climbing up fire escapes, Perry was able to get a look in and find another rubber seal. It was indeed a peephole. They found another peephole in Lily Waters's flat in the bathroom, which again had its own flat roof. Mia Xien lived in an upper flat and had a roof over the entire accommodation. When up there, it took Perry a while before he found the rubber seal. It looked down straight into her bathroom. Pauline Drummond also had an upper flat. Once again, there was a peephole in the bathroom.

'So, they could see everyone,' said Perry, standing with Susan on the roof of Lily Waters's flat.

'You could see the bath with the women so clearly. It's a sexual thing,' said Susan, 'wanting to see the women in the nude.'

'But James's is in the living room,' said Perry.

'More to watch him. See what he's doing. Only place you can get one in as well,' said Susan. 'If you think about it, everywhere else in his flat has got a roof above it.'

'But that's true of some of the women,' said Perry. 'Some of their flats. You can only get a peep into the bathroom.'

'That's handy, isn't it,' said Susan. 'Somebody up there enjoying themselves?'

They next checked Georgie Mackie's accommodation. It was bigger, with plenty of access onto the roof. Perry was stunned when he found a small hole above her bathroom. Another rubber cover was in place.

'Forensics would have been in here, wouldn't they?'

'Yes,' said Susan. 'At least for a quick check. They haven't been into James's yet.'

'So that would explain them missing the peephole in James's flat. But how did they miss this one?'

Susan went off to talk to Jona, while Perry made his way on to the deputy headmistress's accommodation. And there in the bathroom was another peephole. As Perry stood on the roof looking down into the bathroom, Jona climbed the emergency escape with Susan and joined him.

'How did you miss it?' asked Perry.

'I don't think we did. We don't miss things like that,' said Jona.

'Well, the hole's there. Is it recent?' asked Perry.

'I can't tell that. You could look at water ingress, but there has been none. It won't be if people are having baths, maybe, but it takes time. It'd have to have been there for six months, a year depending of course on how much steam is in that room. I'd have difficulty trying to say when it was cut,' said Jona. 'We could try to check. It's not going to be easy, and to be honest, we've got quite a few other things we're trying to do at the moment. I'm quite stretched.'

'In terms of cutting one of these, what do you need?'

'Simple drill, come in from the top by the looks of it. These rubber seals, you can get them just about anywhere. Probably bought with cash. Then you don't have to leave a trace.'

'Okay,' said Perry. 'So we've got all these peepholes. Someone is enjoying themselves by looking at the women in the bath and then watching James.'

'And they see Georgie in with James. That's why James is a traitor and Georgie's a slut,' said Susan.

'It's a bit simple, isn't it?' said Perry.

'Sometimes it is that simple,' said Jona.

'You've not met Donnie,' said Perry. 'I'm not convinced.'

'If it were a janitor, he'd have the tools to do this,' said Jona. 'But then anybody might have the tools to do this. It doesn't need much. They could always borrow his, I guess. There's nothing special about these peepholes.'

'There's another thing,' said Perry.

'What?' asked Susan.

'I say this as a man,' said Perry. 'Don't come after me, okay? But put yourself in the mind of someone wanting to look,' he said. 'Iris Adams. Young woman. She's only twenty-eight. Good body. Absolutely. You want to look. Mia Zen. Again, absolutely. Lily Waters. Yes. Pauline Drummond even. She's not that old. Yeah. Absolutely. Have a look. Georgie. Stunner. Absolutely. But Mrs Fotheringham-Smythe? No.'

Susan looked at Perry, almost with annoyance.

'Don't shoot the messenger,' said Perry. 'I mean, you'd have to have a fetish for an older woman, as well as hungering after the younger form.'

'That's a terrible thing to say,' said Susan.

'It is,' said Jona. 'Might also be accurate, though.'

'Some men like older,' said Susan.

'It's all a bit . . . well . . .' mused Perry. 'Why also just here?

There're loads of other rooms. I take it Donnie would have access to just about anywhere. You've got . . . forgive me,' said Perry, and he almost looked a little embarrassed saying this, 'but if you're that pervert, if you're wanting to sit there and ogle nude women in the bath or whatever, why don't you stick one in the changing room showers? You've got all these teen girls running around.'

'That's true,' said Jona. 'Maybe he just likes the older woman.'

'Not that old,' said Susan. 'Twenty-eight. And Perry's right, there are other members of staff. Do we check around there? Do we check the showers?'

'I think we check,' said Jona. 'That would make sense, wouldn't it?'

It took another hour, but when they gathered again, there was no sign of any other peepholes. They checked Donnie's too, and his lodge had nothing. He did, however, have ladders; he had drills. He had all the equipment to do this. There were also black rubber stoppers, the same as were found on the roof. They were in the school stores.

'So that's where they're coming from,' said Perry.

'But you and I are standing looking at this. It's not closed. Anyone could grab those,' said Susan.

'Yes, you're right,' said Perry. 'Who would want to see all the senior staff? Why the bathroom? We're assuming a sexual agenda. Maybe it's just a way of listening in. Maybe it's a way of keeping track.'

'Surely there's a better way of doing that,' said Jona.

'With some of these roofs, that's the only access in.'

'But the ones where it isn't are still in the bathroom with the ladies,' said Susan.

'Well, Donnie's definitely needs looked at further,' said Perry.

'The big boss is going to want that. But I've already met him. Maybe we get a different angle on this. Someone to ask him slightly different questions.'

'Who?' said Susan.

'I'll see if Ross will talk to him. See if the Sarge will do it.'

'Good idea,' said Susan.

'I'll go find him,' said Perry.

Chapter 17

Alan Ross made his way over to Donnie's lodge, keen to talk to the man for several reasons. Perry had been talking about peepholes, and certainly that was something that Donnie needed to be questioned about. However, there was only circumstantial evidence to say that it was he who had cut these peepholes. He'd never been seen doing it, never been caught in the act. And Perry certainly had reservations about why Donnie would do it.

But Ross wanted to speak to him about other things. The buildings that were now empty, and what was inside which had been cleared away. Jona had flagged those up and Ross wasn't happy about them. Something wasn't making sense. Donnie was in the workshop, fixing a toilet seat, when Ross arrived.

'I'm DC Alan Ross with the police. I'd like to ask you a few questions, Donnie.'

'That other man, Perry, he asked me questions.'

'That's right. I'd like to ask you a few more, if that's okay.'

'Can I fix this first?' said Donnie. Ross was watching the man kneeling at a workbench. There had been a break in a fixture for a toilet seat, and Donnie was replacing it. Ross stepped back and indicated the man should continue. Two minutes later, Donnie looked satisfied with his work.

'I can put the toilet seat back on after you talk to me,' he said. 'Would you like a cup of tea? I'm having tea.'

'Okay,' said Ross, and the two men sat down in the workshop after Donnie had boiled the kettle.

'Donnie,' said Ross, 'do you know anything about holes cut into the bathrooms of some of the senior staff?'

'No,' said Donnie.

'We found holes cut into the bathrooms of Lily Waters, Mia Zenn, Iris Adams, Pauline Drummond, the deputy Headmistress, and Georgie Mackie's too. Do you know anything about their being there? Have you ever noticed anything when you've been doing maintenance?'

'There are no holes in there. I was on the roofs not that long ago. There are no holes.'

'They were sealed up with one of those rubber covers,' said Ross. 'Let me have a look. Yes, over there. There's some of them. They were put on top.'

'They would keep the rain out. You could lift it off easily,' said Donnie. 'It's a good idea.'

'It's a good idea to have a peephole in the people's bathrooms? You'll be able to see the women in the bath.'

'If that's what you wanted to do,' said Donnie, 'you could do that. But why? Why? Why would you want to see them in the bath? You couldn't talk to them.'

'No, Donnie, you couldn't. I think it's for a different reason.'

Donnie looked slightly bemused, but then he turned and just smiled.

'The buildings that were cleared out, Donnie. My friends say that you didn't get into them. They were locked. You didn't go into them. You didn't open them up during the day.'

'No, they were always locked. Not part of my duties. They're empty now.'

'What happened to them, Donnie?'

'Cleared. Health and safety. The deputy headmistress would know.'

'Did you clear them?'

'No,' said Donnie. 'Outside company. I wasn't involved. Nothing to do with Donnie.'

'Why? Why weren't you involved? Surely, if it was something being moved or adapted on this site, surely you would be involved. No?'

'I said I could help. I have lots of tools, but they said no. There was asbestos. They said Donnie couldn't touch asbestos. And they were right. I can't touch asbestos. I looked it up. Not good stuff. You don't go near it. So the company did it.'

'Do you know who they were?' asked Ross.

'I wasn't told, but they had a van that said Buchan and Co. on the side. Glasgow. It said Glasgow.'

'Were they okay?'

'I didn't see them. They came in at night.'

'They arrived late at night?'

'Did all their work at night,' said Donnie. 'No one allowed near it. Not even standing outside. Big cordon around it. They came in, they cleared everything, and they went. Then suddenly everything was open.'

'And you didn't have to, what, do anything?'

'No.'

'Donnie, when somebody comes to work here, do they have to sign in? Do they have to sign a permit?'

'Yes. They come to see me, and I take them, and they sign

into the book over here.'

'Okay. And those are permits to work, yes? Do they need permits to work?'

'Yes, I say it's okay. And I sign this bit,' said Donnie.

'But what about this one with the asbestos? Would not you have to sign the permit to work?'

'No. Headmistress did that. Miss Georgie told me not to worry.'

'But the permit, do you have a book somewhere with them all written in?' asked Ross. 'Lever arch files maybe? Something like that?'

Donnie got up, walked over to a folder on a shelf, pulled it out, and came back and sat beside Ross. He opened it up.

'Here are the permits.' He flicked through. 'There's the permit for them. See? Signed by the headmistress, not by me.'

'And tags and that for working?'

'Handed out by the headmistress.'

'So that's the record of what they did.'

'Yes,' said Donnie. 'See, it says asbestos.' Ross flicked the permit over and behind it was a work method for removing asbestos. It all seemed okay.

'But why at night?' he asked.

'I don't know,' said Donnie. 'Wasn't allowed near it. Maybe it was safer. Maybe because everyone would be inside. No dust. But you have to use special methods.'

'And it took how long to clear?'

'Couple of days, but they worked every night. So I should say a couple of nights.'

'Thank you, Donnie,' said Ross, and sipped down the tea. He wasn't a big fan of tea, but he would not put extra pressure on the man when he'd offered tea. Ross went to leave and then stopped and turned and looked back at Donnie. He didn't look the type to go staring at nude women.

Ross quickly glanced around the workshop. There were none of those calendars either, either the simply scantily clad ones or the outright nudes that you sometimes found in male workspaces. These days were of course different from twenty, thirty years ago, but they still existed in the right places. This was Donnie's workshop. He could have had something hung up, even a movie poster . There was nothing that showed anything to suggest that Donnie was interested in the opposite sex. Ross found that strange if he was someone who was ogling them at night or looking into their bathrooms.

Ross made his way back to the room they were working from in the school. He looked up Buchan and Co. in Glasgow, and they did indeed do asbestos removal amongst other works. There would be forms that went along with it, forms for disposal. Ross might get a look at those.

He called up the local council asking about the disposal of asbestos. After going through different offices, he was put in touch with an environmental officer. He explained that all the paperwork had been done and, yes indeed, there had been asbestos removed. Ross sat back. Asbestos had come out, and asbestos had been put away, but they'd worked through the night. It was unusual. Something bothered Ross about that.

He got up and made his way over to the school offices, finding the deputy headmistress's office. He knocked on the door. She was inside and advised him to come in, in the way that teachers talk to pupils. Ross stood before her desk. She didn't stand up and greet him; rather, she remained at her desk and looked at him with a stare that deserved a pair of glasses to look over.

'How can I help you? Sergeant, isn't it?'

'Yes, it's DS Ross. I was just talking about when you had the buildings gutted that are on the far side of the school. Donnie advised me that mostly it was done at night.'

'Yes, asbestos removal. We thought it quite dangerous, myself and the headmistress. The headmistress said that it would be better if it were done at night. It cost a bit more, but it meant that all the young people were inside. Everyone was out of the way, just in case something happened.'

'Not normal, though, is it?' said Ross. 'Bit of an over-precaution.'

'Well, you may think so, but we think a lot of our young women here, and we're keen to keep them safe. Georgie especially, God rest her soul. That's the way she was.'

'And you had a Glasgow company come in to do it.'

'Well, you couldn't have Donnie doing stuff like that. It had to be done properly by professionals.'

'And they were okay with doing it at night. They didn't advise that it would be better during the day or that.'

'No. They came in and they cleared it.'

'What was in there before?' asked Ross.

'Not much. Just some old equipment. Chairs, tables. But it all went. With the asbestos being dealt with, we thought it best to clear the place.'

'It was locked before, was it?'

'We knew about the asbestos problem for a while. It was just taking time to put in place a method to get it sorted.'

'Did you put up any warning signs? Especially when you found the asbestos.'

'Better not to make anyone aware and panic,' said Mrs

Fotheringham-Smythe. 'Keep it quiet, get it dealt with, and move on. That's the way I saw it, and the way that the headmistress saw it, too.'

'Tell me about Donnie. How do you find him?' asked Ross.

'Janitor. Poor soul. Not quite with us completely, is he? Apparently now he may have been spying on us, too.'

'Do you find he ever looks at you in a strange way?'

'Who knows what Donnie thinks, or how he looks? You think you know people, but then you don't know what's going on behind. I suppose if Georgie was having relations with James, or maybe even just going to James's, and if Donnie was staring at people through these peepholes, maybe he felt like he owned them. And then somebody else, maybe it's just an embrace, maybe it's just a friendly thing in someone's living room.'

'Big jump to murder them and call them a slut, though,' said Ross.

'Nobody really knows what Donnie thinks or how he works. That's the trouble when you think of simple souls, though, isn't it,' said Mrs Fotheringham-Smythe.

'Most of the simple souls I've come across,' said Ross, 'are that—simple souls. Thank you for your time.'

Ross left, but he wasn't happy. The buildings were still bothering him. Why at night? Who in their right mind would want the asbestos removal at night? No one would see. Everyone would be asleep. Ross wondered. The building was locked up, but with no signs saying asbestos. Surely you would have put a big 'keep out' sign up, and put a perimeter around it, more so if it was asbestos.

You wouldn't want anyone getting in there accidentally, or kids sneaking in for cigarettes, like Jona had found. You couldn't have that if it were asbestos. And if they saw it, if they saw that it was a risk to their health, they'd hide somewhere else, surely. You'd scream it. You'd tell everyone. And then get it dealt with.

Ross walked around the school grounds. He felt something was forming, and he couldn't get his head around what it was. So many people from the Glasgow area, school trips to Glasgow. There was something deep in his gut that was saying, we need to look at this more; we need to get more into this. The push for Donnie, Donnie as a suspect, was wrong. Donnie seemed to be the last person.

The only thing that may have actually clicked was the fact that Donnie would be methodical in the way he worked. He was a simple person. But even that worked against him as a suspect. While you could say Donnie could plan how to put somebody in a sexual position, would he? Would he also have the know-how with the drugs? Would he have the strength on his own?

There was also the girl in town, Keira, pregnant by one of the electrician boys. But the school helped her out so much. They keep her local and they keep her in a flat. There was too much here, thought Ross. *Too much. Things weren't sitting comfortably. Yet, at times, they sat too comfortably.*

He'd been to too many murders. He'd seen too much. To wrap Donnie up as the person doing this was so simple but too easy. How to prove it, anyway.

He turned and looked at the school building. *A private school. An academy out here. Sixteen to eighteen-year olds. All the way out in Applecross. Why? Wouldn't you have gone and put it in the middle of Glasgow? Most of them were from Glasgow after all. I suppose they would have said they would have taken them here to give them a unique environment. Take them away from that.*

Why here? It was out of the way. It was somewhere that you didn't pass through. You would go to here by design. Out here, you would be left unbothered. Ross froze suddenly. Left unbothered. That seemed to be important. Something about that phrase. He was getting somewhere. He wondered.

Chapter 18

Susan Cunningham drove into Applecross and down to Keira Saunders' house. She wasn't there to visit Keira. Instead, Ross had asked her to do a bit of snooping around the neighbours to get a feel for Keira Saunders from the outside. They had the idea that the school had helped her. The idea of a woman who'd made a mistake and now was being helped to make her life good again. But everything was coming from the point of view of the school and Keira. Ross had an uneasy feeling, and he wanted something to substantiate that. He told Susan to dig, find out what she could about the life of Keira Saunders.

Susan parked a little distance from Keira's and then approached the street. She tried to stay out of view of Keira's, but it wasn't easy. However, the woman wasn't at her window. And so, Susan began knocking on the neighbour's doors. Two of them weren't in. One didn't even know who lived across the road. But then, directly opposite Kiera's, she knocked the door. The neighbour that came seemed a promising bet. It was a little old dear, as her grandmother would have put it. Susan thought she might be on to a winner.

'Hello? Yes?'

'Hi, I'm DC Susan Cunningham.' Susan pulled out her credentials and held them up for the woman.

'You're a policewoman, dear.'

'Yes, that's right.'

'No uniform. You really should have a uniform.'

'I'm a detective. I'm a detective from Inverness.'

'Detective.' The woman took the credentials and stared at them.

'You can phone if you wish. Call the nearest station. Ask about me.'

'It's okay, dearie. Come in.' The woman gave the credentials back to Susan, who stepped into the house and had the door closed after her.

'Can I ask your name?' asked Susan.

'I'm Annie. Annie. Just call me Annie.'

'And your surname, Annie?'

'Oh, this'll be for the official bit, won't it? Anne. Anne Jefferson.'

'Thank you, Annie.'

'Come through here, dear. Come through here.' Annie led Susan through into her living room, where a large bay window looked straight across the street towards the flat of Kiera Saunders.

'Is this about those boys at the centre?' asked Annie.

'No. No, it's not. What boys?'

'I saw them painting things on the wall. Those cans. They had those cans.'

'No, Annie, that's not to do with that.'

'You'll have tea, dear, won't you?'

'I'm fine. I'm on duty, Annie.'

'No, dear. Sit down.' Susan felt herself being placed into

a seat and relented. 'Lovely girl, aren't you? I mean, you've got a lovely figure. And that hair. You shouldn't tie it up in a ponytail. You should let your hair out.'

'I'm working, Annie. I don't leave my hair out when I'm working.'

'Have you got a man?'

'No, Annie.'

'That is strange.' And the woman went off into the kitchen. She came back five minutes later. A pot of tea, two cups and a tray, and a large cake.

'Can I cut you some?'

'No, no.' And then Susan relented. She thought of Perry. Perry read people, and Perry got alongside people. Maybe she needed to do the same.

'I'll have a slice, please. Shall I pour the tea?'

'Oh, yes,' said Annie. 'Absolutely.'

Susan cut two large slices of cake, placed one over beside Annie's chair, and sat down with her own. Annie handed her a cup of tea, complete with saucer and cup, and they sat back. Annie stared out the window.

'What do you do, Annie?'

'Oh, I'm retired, dear. Retired a while ago.'

Susan thought she should have phrased that better. 'What does your day consist of?'

'Me? Oh. Well, Mondays, we go down to the church. There's a lunch club. And then on Wednesdays, they take me out to get my shopping. On Thursday morning, that's when the cleaning comes in the afternoon. I'm usually here, and my friend comes over for a chat. Friday, my family picks me up around tea time. We go for a chippy tea. And then on Saturday—Saturday I'm often out. My daughter takes me shopping. And then on

Sunday, it's church in the morning and then in the evening, there's a little fellowship group I go to. Often it's here.'

'Do you know the woman across the street from you?'

'Which one?' asked Annie.

Of course, there was a set of flats. 'The pregnant young lady.'

'Oh, Keira,' said Annie. 'I know Keira.'

'How do you find her?' asked Susan.

'Good looking girl. Young though. Way too young for a baby. Got pregnant up at the school. That's what they said.'

'Do you know who the father is?'

'They say it's one of the boys. But he's dead now. There was an accident. A crash. And the driver drove off. He came off his bike. Terrible.'

'Did you see him?'

'I didn't see him much here,' said Annie. 'Not a lot. Sometimes. When they knew she was pregnant and they moved in, yes.'

'Did she get many other visitors?' asked Susan.

'Well, you see, I sit here most days. I like the window. You see people. You see everybody come and go. I see everybody who comes and goes from Kiera's. Do you know who comes and goes the most?'

'No,' said Susan. 'Who?'

'The postman. That's who. Always the postman or those delivery drivers. That's who comes and goes the most. That girl, and I know this because some of my friends have said it, pleads poverty. She's got no money. But all the time, boxes were arriving. Sometimes furniture. Sometimes it's food, some expensive food. I think there's been some cosmetics. I know because the driver came to give me something, and he gave me the wrong box initially, and I said, no that's over the road, but it was cosmetics.'

'They weren't for you then?' said Susan.

'Oh no, dear. I don't use any, not anymore, none of that sort. My days of that are gone, long gone.'

'You think she's well off?'

'Apparently, her parents don't want to know. That's what I heard,' said Annie. 'That's what's on the grapevine. But somebody does. Somebody's sending her stuff. They don't take it; they send it to her. There's only one man who brings her anything.'

'Oh yes? She gets other visitors then?'

'Two. Well, there was one young man, but he hasn't been recently. I say recently in the last four or five days. He came all the time, very young, great body. I may not be out there anymore, but I can still spot a good body,' laughed Annie. 'Very trim, lovely bottom.' Susan nearly laughed out loud, but she told Annie to continue.

'He used to come and never brought anything. He brought nothing and he would come and stay for a while.'

Susan wondered. She reached into her jacket and pulled out some photographs. The first one she had was James. It was the school photo from the previous year. She stood up and gave it to Annie.

'Oh, that's him. Lovely bottom. Absolutely lovely bottom. He came along, and he would stay for quite a while and go again. She was always glad to see him.'

'How do you know?'

'She was at the window. At the window waiting for him to come,' said Annie.

'So she knew he was coming.'

'Oh yes, he wasn't just dropping in. She knew he was coming.

Ready for him. Not her man, the one that died. But I guess she's pregnant, she's got a kid. Probably wants somebody to help her through life. I will not judge but I think she was, well, enticing him in that way. He always looked a bit dishevelled.'

Susan nodded. There was something very engaging about Annie. Yes, she was an old woman, but she had a life and soul in her that wasn't yet dead. Almost a mischievous grin at the way she said things.

'So, anybody else apart from this man?'

'There was another one. He was different. He would come with flowers, you know? Fruit. Like you would visit somebody in a hospital. That's what it looked like. If you didn't know it was homes, you would think he was going to the hospital. Flowers wrapped up in that way. Fruit in a paper bag. The sort of thing you would bring to somebody who wasn't well.

'To be honest, when I looked at him, I thought he looked quite simple. Had that walk, you know? Just as if the world around wasn't happening. Just walking along, happy. I was going to say fat, dumb and happy, but he wasn't fat. I'm not sure he was dumb. Certainly happy. Simple. Not dumb.'

Susan reached inside her jacket and pulled out Donnie's photograph from the school records. She walked over and gave it to Annie.

'That's him. Nice face in some ways. Simple but pleasant face.'

'Did she know he was coming?' asked Susan.

'She was never looking out the window when he arrived. Never stood there waiting for him. The other guy, I could have told you the other guy was coming because she was looking. But she hasn't been looking out the window in a few days now.'

'How long did the second guy stay?'

'Not that long. Maybe an hour. The other guy, hours. Sometimes three.'

'Did he ever stay the night?' asked Susan.

'No. Did visit at times at odd hours. He would normally visit after teatime, which is normal because most people would be at work. On a Saturday, maybe, or Sunday, he would visit earlier. I know twice he visited sort of eight, nine o'clock at night then didn't leave until midnight.'

'Well, thank you Annie, you've been a great help.'

'You really want to know what I think?'

'Go on,' said Susan.

'I think she's a little minx.'

Susan swallowed hard. She was half wondering, half nervous about what would come out next. But there was no way she was going to miss what Annie had to say.

'She's a little minx. She got herself pregnant up the road at that school. Now she's come down, and the lad, God rest his soul, has died. So, she's decided she needs somebody else. Difficult when you're in that state. Some men like that, don't they? I've seen enough in this life to know that some men like that. Some men find pregnancy very attractive. Puts others off. Put my Gerald off. Let me tell you that. It was annoying, though. I wasn't put off. Only had two kids. I would not go through all that again. Not when he looked at me as if I were something wrong then.'

Susan thought she was getting a little too much detail and quietly finished the rest of her cake. She went to stand, but Annie put her hand up.

'Now listen to me,' she said. 'The thing I've got a problem with is my friend Elsie.'

'Elsie?' said Susan.

'Elsie. She comes here on a Sunday night for the group but Elsie's from London, and Elsie said to me she wasn't convinced that girl got pregnant by that bloke, the boy from the electricians.'

'Why not? asked Susan. How does Elsie know?'

'Elsie's got her ear to the ground. Also, that guy you've got the photograph of from the school. The young lad with the nice bottom. He was here and visiting while her bloke was still alive. I talked with Elsie about this. That don't seem right. That seems to say something else.'

'And how often was he here?'

'When she first moved down, he would come. And maybe, oh, well actually, I remember when she moved in and her man had helped her and stuff, he went away about nine o'clock. He's probably getting up for work the next morning. Ten o'clock that night, the guy from your photograph arrives, leaves two hours later.'

'And how long was that after she moved in?'

'She'd been in less than a week.'

'Really?' said Susan.

'Yes, less than a week. I don't blame her, though. You know, if I were in that situation, pregnant, especially now, and had two on the go, and one's gone, well, you've got to hang on to the other one, haven't you? Guess that's the way it is. Oh, she'll know the jib of it anyway soon. They don't always look at you the same when you've got a wee one. That's the trouble, isn't it? Men are really just big babies. When you've got a baby of your own, you haven't got time to look after them and they get fed up with you.'

Susan felt there was another involved rail coming out and she'd got out of Annie what she needed.

153

'Well, thank you for the tea and the cake. I've got to get back to my inspector. He'll be needing me.'

'Oh, come again, love. Anything else you need to know? Annie's here.'

Susan nodded. *Absolutely*, she thought. *Annie would be here.* But Annie had given her something that nobody else could. Ross's hunch had been right. There was something up. She'd go back now and let everyone know what she'd found out.

Chapter 19

Macleod was almost livid. He'd spent a couple of hours with the senior staff and got nowhere. Apparently, they'd all been together. They'd all been together waiting for James. James hadn't come. They alibied each other as being in the staff room. Not one of them was missing. Not one of them was elsewhere. He'd gone from having a possibility of every one of the senior staff being a potential suspect for Georgie Mackie's murder to having none of them. They were all together when James would have been immobilised and then killed.

He would have to start again, and because of that, he was pulling the team in. They needed different angles, of course. Donnie hadn't been at the staff meeting. Donnie had been off on his routine tasks. It was just that at the time in which he was doing his routine task, it took him to one of the septic tanks, which meant that nobody had seen Donnie.

Donnie had the opportunity to kill James. It seemed a huge ask to Macleod, but everything was pointing towards Donnie. Either that or Macleod would have to fish beyond the senior team. There were three hundred schoolgirls here, three hundred schoolgirls, each with an opportunity to find a problem with Georgie Mackie. Did she have relations with James? Is that what was annoying people? Is that what was kicking it all off? Had James been with any of the girls?

But then to see a group of schoolgirls—because it would have to be a group, surely, to subdue somebody like James, or even Georgie—kill them in that way would be incredibly enterprising. It was meant to be an academy for gifted women, but Macleod couldn't see it. It might mean he'd have to interview the schoolgirls, and he didn't want that. Macleod struggled with that age. He just didn't connect with them. Part of his annoyance was Hope not being here, not being available.

There was a knock on the door, and Jona entered looking around her. 'Just me, is it?'

'They're coming. They'll be here in a minute. I'll put coffee on.'

'Excellent,' said Jona. 'I fancy a coffee. Been busy. My team is spread out. We've been checking your peepholes. There's nothing there to be found. We're struggling.'

'Don't go any further,' said Macleod. 'Wait for the team to get here.'

Susan and Perry arrived next, followed by Ross and the team sat down together around a small table, coffee in hand.

'You started before they arrived, Jona. Recap and tell everyone what's going on at your end.'

'First off,' said Jona, 'both victims were immobilised by injection and then they were poisoned. The poison is subtle, does not make any sudden jerks within the body. This is important because they've put them in a position to be held in. You don't want the body to react.'

'Sorry,' said Perry.

'What they've done in killing these two people is actually

quite ingenious. And I say that without wanting to. They've managed to balance them into a sexual position with a mannequin. But to get into that position and to maintain that position after death with no other supports, you need to get the body set up so that the centre of gravity of the body is maintained within the structure. Then the body doesn't tip.'

'Put that in English for me,' said Susan.

'Basically, get the body in a position and hold that position while the body dies. Then, allow rigor mortis to set in and then detach anything holding that body in place. The body's got to be in a fairly stable position to begin with.'

'So what, they set them up like a Subbuteo player?'

'Yeah, like a miniature. Susan, that's right,' said Jona.

'What about the poisons and about the substance that makes the victim immobilised?' asked Perry.

'I'm still getting the lab test run. But even if I don't know what the substance is, to deliver a substance like that in the right dose, you need to know what you're about. Also, everything is clean. Around the murder sites, everything is clean. You need to know how to keep everything clean or how to tidy it up afterwards. And it is tidied up to my level.'

'So then,' said Macleod, 'you'd have to have that person. The only person at that level we know of is Lily. Lily Waters. She's a former forensic officer.'

'I was looking into that,' said Jona. 'I thought I'd have a word with some of my colleagues. She was good, clever. She'd certainly have the level of ability.'

'Well, that's something,' said Macleod. 'What about the actual death? Could you do it as one person? Do you need more than one person?'

'Be tough,' said Jona. 'I wouldn't want to. It'd be tough to do it as one person, and if you did, you'd have to surprise them to immobilise them. Maybe sneak up on them. Otherwise, you'd have to physically take a hold of them.'

'So it'd be easier with more than one person?' asked Macleod.

'It would be easier,' confirmed Jona. 'Remember, they didn't get James set up perfectly. He had extra supporting wires.'

'Donnie's quite strong,' said Ross. 'As much as I don't think it's him, he's strong.'

'He is that,' said Perry. 'A powerful guy.'

'So,' said Macleod, 'what about the peepholes?'

'Well, anybody could have made them,' said Jona. 'I can't say how recently they were. They're certainly not very old, but I couldn't turn around and say with absolute confidence that they're less than six months old. However, we didn't see any at Georgie Mackie's lodgings. We're thorough. We don't miss that.'

'So what, the peepholes have only just been put in?' asked Macleod.

'Georgie Mackie's peephole is definitely new, since we arrived,' said Jona. 'I'll stake my reputation on it. My people are not sloppy.'

'Of course not,' said Macleod. 'Does that mean the other ones are new? Then why? Is Donnie being framed?'

'Think about the peephole,' said Perry, 'because I don't think Donnie did it. You just need a ladder and a drill to do those peepholes, and access to the rubber blanks that were put in to cover them up. Correct?'

Jona nodded. 'Anybody could do it. Any idiot,' said Jona. 'You could do it,' she said to Macleod. He reeled a little. 'Well, you could. At the end of the day, you're not the greatest handyman around, are you?'

'So,' said Macleod, 'what's the point, Perry?'

'Well, think about it. They say Donnie can do it, yeah? But you have to do it while the flats are empty. You have to get there when nobody else is in. Now, the reason that points to Donnie is that he's going about his business during the day and everybody else is working. But that is a very tough ask. How do you know when people are coming back? Or do they?'

'There's another thing about Kiera Jackson,' said Susan. 'I went down to see Kiera's neighbours. A little old lady across the road, she spotted visitors ever since Keira went there. There was the young lad that she was with who then died in the road accident. He would obviously come in every now and again, and that was perfectly normal. James, however, started visiting her soon after she was moved down there. Another person who came to visit her was Donnie.'

'You what?' blurted Perry.

'Donnie visited her. Comes down with fruit, comes down with flowers. But the woman said to me, bizarrely, it was like he was going to visit somebody in hospital the way he turned up. James used to come down after school had finished. Sometimes he would stay for a couple of hours. Donnie's visit was quicker.'

'I think there's possibly another line of attack here too,' said Ross. 'I've been looking at those empty buildings. They were said to have had asbestos in them. Now I've checked, and there's been asbestos given to waste authorities. All the paperwork's correct. But all the work was done at night. Donnie didn't sign off any permits for that one. They're all done by Georgie. A firm came up from Glasgow. Glasgow is in everything around here; a lot of the girls come from Glasgow; trips go to Glasgow; they go to the big cities; a lot of the staff are up from Glasgow.'

'Well, Glasgow is pretty close,' said Perry, 'in its defence.'

'Yes, it is, but so is Inverness, so is Edinburgh, so why are so many from Glasgow? A lot of them from Glasgow are here on scholarship; the ones not from Glasgow, and a few others are from paying families.'

'It's a bit tenuous,' said Macleod.

'Yes, that would be tenuous. But look at the trips away. They go away on trips. They go to Inverness, they go to Glasgow, they go to Edinburgh. Now the trips look like they're good educational trips. They're off to museums, they're off to the theatre, they're off to institutions. All solid educational stuff.'

'So what's the problem?' asked Macleod.

'Certain girls are on all the trips,' said Ross.

'How do you know this?' asked Macleod.

'Because I use a laptop,' said Ross. 'What I've been doing is cross-referencing and using all the information the school has about their trips to see who's gone where. By cross-referencing and using my spreadsheets, I can tell you that certain girls are there all the time on the trips. You wouldn't notice it looking at it, but when you collate it, it's there.'

'And these girls are?'

'They're all from Madson House. It's one of the houses within the school. With the other three houses, the girls are not always there, but Madson House, all board together as well.'

'One of the junior teachers,' said Ross, 'told me that when they go on the trips, they go in houses. They don't go by age. So, although the other houses go on the trips, some of these trips are Madson House on their own. I also talked to Glasgow and to drug enforcement. The school trips matched

160

up with drug shipments into the city at a rate of seventy per cent. School trips from Madson house, ninety per cent.'

'So Madson go on their own?' said Macleod.

'No, no. It's much more subtle,' said Ross. 'You get one of the other houses going with them, so half the school's away. But every time there was a serious drug shipment reported on drug movements in the cities, ninety per cent of the time Madson were on a school trip to that city. That's significant.'

'You can't be suggesting,' said Susan, 'that the girls are running drugs, that we've got a cartel of young people.'

'I don't know what I'm suggesting. I'm just telling you what the facts say.'

'Anything else to back it up?' asked Macleod.

'Yes, sir,' said Ross. 'When the girls come, they get new bags. There are always new bags given to them. And these are for trips away.'

'And only Madson get these?' asked Macleod.

'No, everybody gets these.'

Macleod sat back, sipping his coffee. 'Seems to me that there's a lot going on here that we don't yet understand. We're being sold a story, possibly. But we need to make sure the story is false. So at the moment, we monitor Donnie. So, Perry, I need you to speak to Donnie about his trips to see Kiera and about the peepholes. See if we've got a sexual element to him.'

'I didn't find that when I spoke to him,' said Ross.

'Nor me,' said Perry. 'But I'll double-check. I'll push.'

'Do,' said Macleod. 'We need to be sure he's not involved in this. He's just a cover story.'

'I need to be getting up the road to work on the bodies,' said Jona.

'You do that,' said Macleod. 'When you get something, tell

161

me.' Macleod turned and looked at Ross. 'It's good, Alan, the angle you're coming from. But there's not enough there to go at anything. So, we will not bring that up. We will not question people here. I want you to go to Glasgow, and I want you to push the bag and the trip angle. I want you also to track the builders in Glasgow. Find out if there's anything dodgy about them.'

'Don't you want me to stay and supervise?'

'No,' said Macleod. 'I can do that. I've got Perry here and I've got Susan. It's not a problem. We've got how many uniforms protecting the site? This is your angle. You said to me you were good at it, and you are, and you've done it. This is you solving the case your way. Fine. It's not what I would have you do or have a sergeant doing, but it's what you're doing and it's working. So, we chase it. You chase it. You're the one who understands it. Go find me that link. Go and find it. Explain it to me. Show me why it actually is real and not just a set of coincidences on your laptop.'

'Yes, sir,' said Ross. He was almost beaming.

'And Susan, I want you to go see Keira, and I want you to talk to her about the men meeting her. We need to find out just what she is. She's pregnant. We can't ask the would-be father if it's his, though I suspect it might not be. He could be the father, and he may have been having an affair with her. He may have thought he got her pregnant, which is why he kept visiting her until he suddenly died in a road accident. And the person who killed him drives off and doesn't stay behind. You need to find out what James was to her and also what Donnie is. She's a pregnant woman. She's got a lot of needs in terms of where she stays, where she lives, and support.'

'Oh, she's getting that,' said Susan. 'Annie said she gets all sorts of stuff through, says the delivery drivers are one of the biggest visitors to her.'

'Then find out who's giving her stuff,' said Macleod. 'I'll hold fort here. I'll keep this together. You lot get me my answers. Solve this case for me.'

There were nods and another smile from Ross. And soon Macleod was the only one left in the room apart from Jona. She turned to him. 'You okay?'

'Why?' asked Macleod.

'You've just sent them all off to do the digging. You used to do all the digging. Seoras Macleod would have run round.'

'I'm a DCI now in charge of three different divisions. Jona, it's not what I do anymore. I send people out.'

'And how's that working for you?'

Macleod smiled at her. 'You see it, don't you?'

'Seoras, you're bored. You're fed up with this. You don't even want to be here,' said Jona. 'Oh, you're going through the motions. You're doing everything right, and you will solve it. But you would have been down there. You would have been running here, there and everywhere to sort everything out, to dig out the answers, to find everything, to be in the thick of it.'

'I don't get in the thick of it anymore. It's Hope's terrain, and I only do this until Hope comes back. And then I'll give it to Hope and I'll sit up in my office again. I'll sit on top.'

'It's more than that, though.'

'It is,' said Macleod. 'The Forseti group, when they came in that case, they almost killed some of us. They almost took away some of my people. It hit me. It was tough. Suddenly, Anna was involved. Anna Hunt, our secret service head is there, involved in so much, especially the last case. We run things differently than we used to.'

'But what's really up?'

'I'm here,' said Macleod. 'I'm here and Jane is sitting in a lovely house that I have. She hasn't got me and I haven't got her, and by the time I retire, by the time that I get to the end of all of this, who knows what state we're going to be in. Who knows if we could drop dead the next day, because that's the way of it. There's plenty of people get past sixty-five and don't get much further. Plenty of people end up not able to walk. My bones don't feel the same as they used to.'

'And?' said Jona.

'She came all the way up here to be with me. She nearly got thrown into a bath of acid. And she's still here. She's had plenty of other instances where this job has impacted on her, and she's still here. I think I owe it to her to give her some time.'

'You're serious, aren't you?'

'Very,' said Macleod. 'If it wasn't for Hope having a baby, I may even have been gone by now. But I can't go until she's back. I won't leave it like that. This is my team, my people. Same with Emmett. Same with Clarissa. My team, my people, and I'll make sure they've got good people looking after them.'

'And you're sure?'

'Yes,' said Macleod. 'Does it shock you?'

'What, that you make some rational sense? No. The fact that you've put yourself first and not this damn job? Yes,' said Jona. 'Yes, go. You should take that woman and have the best years of your life before you have life no more. Otherwise, what's any of it worth?'

Jona stepped forward, reached up with her hands and pulled Macleod down to her. She kissed him on the forehead. 'Good luck with it all. I won't tell anyone.'

He watched her go. If Hope had been here, he'd have told her. But she wasn't. Jona was doing what she always did. The rock in the chaos. The solid, standing stone that never moved no matter what was going on. He smiled to himself. He hadn't even told Jane yet.

Chapter 20

Alan Ross was up early that morning before driving down to Glasgow. It was a clear and bright morning, if somewhat cold. Not unusual for the time of year, and Ross quite enjoyed the drive down. He was on his own and therefore, didn't have to endure Perry's little foibles that annoyed him, Susan's unbelievably bright optimism or indeed the boss grilling him about what he was on his laptop for this time.

Ross was on his way to kill two birds with one stone. He would visit Buchan and Co. to ask about the removal of asbestos from the outside buildings at the school. He had also identified the manufacturer of the bags that were given to the new arrivals each year. And not just the supplier of them, but rather, the company from Glasgow who made them.

However, his first stop would be Buchan and Co. Using the sat-nav on his phone, Ross entered the busy Glasgow city area before heading through to the south side and an industrial estate. Like most industrial estates, it wasn't glamorous, but there was a high fenced compound with the words Buchan and Co. written above a gate.

Ross parked up and walked through to a reception that had

paper everywhere. The walls had old wood panelling on them, and looked like they'd been there for a while. Behind a desk that was almost too high for her sat an older woman, wrapped up in a cardigan, and only three feet away from a blow heater.

'Excuse me, I was wondering if you could help.'

'Do you have an appointment?'

'No,' said Ross.

'Are you here for work?'

'No,' said Ross.

'Are you looking to purchase anything?'

'No,' said Ross.

'Then what do you want?'

Ross pulled out his credentials, placing them on the desk in front of the lady. 'I am Detective Sergeant Alan Ross.'

'And?' said the woman.

'I'm investigating some deaths at the Applecross Academy for the gifted. Apparently, this company did some work there.'

'Yeah, but that's a little while ago. And?'

'I was told that there was removal of asbestos.'

'Could be,' said the woman.

'I'd like to see the documents relating to the removal of that asbestos.'

'Are you serious?'

'Yes, I am,' Ross advised. 'Very serious.'

'I've got all these requisitions to get through. I've got to pull together invoices for all these companies, and you want me to go racing through asbestos paperwork.'

'You're not digitised.'

'It's partly digitised, love, but it still means I have to hunt. He doesn't file these things properly.'

She turned and looked behind her. There was an entire wall

filled with shelving that held lever arch files. There was some sort of coding system on the outside, but Ross, for the life of him, couldn't tell what any of them meant.

'It's a murder investigation,' said Ross. 'I'd be most obliged if you would find the paperwork for me.'

'Obliged? You'd be obliged, would you? Money, are you?'

'I must insist on seeing those documents,' said Ross.

'I don't know. You're not from the environment or something.'

'I'm a detective sergeant, a police officer on a murder case.'

'Well, I'll get the boss. Hang on.'

The woman disappeared into a back office and then reappeared to sit down at her desk.

'Boss coming?' asked Ross.

'He's just coming. He's been on the crapper.'

There was nothing like class, thought Ross to himself. He stood there waiting for two minutes until a man emerged from the back room. He was in a tatty shirt, his grey hair slicked over to one side, and a cigarette hung from his mouth. Clearly, he wasn't interested in the idea of not smoking indoors.

'What the hell do you want?'

Ross felt obliged to pull out his credentials again. 'Detective Sergeant Alan Ross. I am looking for your asbestos removal documentation regarding the job you did at Applecross Academy for the gifted.'

'Really?'

'Yes, specifically the asbestos removal documentation.' The man stood there shaking his head. 'What's the matter?' asked Ross. 'Don't you have it?'

'There weren't any, were there?'

'What do you mean?' asked Ross.

'Oh, we took some stuff out of there. Took it, shifted it downtown. Or rather, we disconnected some stuff, and we placed it into some vans that went downtown. But there was no asbestos. Headmistress was an idiot.'

'How do you mean?' asked Ross.

'What I just bloody told you? We turned up and there was a load of equipment in there.'

'What sort of equipment?'

'I don't know. Fans, heating, heating elements, sort of tray, bench, table-type things. I don't know exactly what it was for, but anyway, it had to come out before we could then have a look in the roof for the asbestos. You get out what you can first, so you don't cover it when you start removing asbestos. It's not an easy job and she wanted us to do it in the middle of the night.'

'Why?' asked Ross.

'Because the woman was wired to the moon.'

'How did you get the job?' asked Ross.

'Honestly?'

'Well, I'm a detective, so yes, honestly,' said Ross.

'Got sent my way. There's a few people we do jobs for that are, well, a bit on the rough end. If they ask you to do something, you do it. I mean, they pay well, but, yeah, they're a bit on the—'

'On the dodgy side,' said Ross. 'The ones you don't want to disappoint.'

'Exactly. Not that we do anything illegal for them, but when they ask, well, yeah, you say you'll do it. And they pay above the rate, so . . .'

'I understand,' said Ross. 'So, they asked you to go up there.'

'Exactly, to a school. Seemed strange, but anyway, we got

up there, and we have to move this equipment out. She says, we'll do it in the middle of the night, because that way it won't disturb anyone. And it'll be safer doing the asbestos at night.'

'So what happened?' asked Ross.

'We go in, we shift all this equipment, so you've got an empty building except for what would be the asbestos up in the roof. And we open up the roof and there's none there.'

'Didn't you check before?'

'We were told not to. We were told it would be there by our friends, and therefore we went and did it. I called them up afterwards and said, Look, there's no asbestos there because I didn't want to get in trouble. I didn't want them thinking I'd done a rubbish job for them.'

'Fair enough,' said Ross. 'And then what?'

'They said that's fine. Said the woman must have made a mistake—not to worry about it. Got paid. And then, well, just got on with things.'

'Do you have any documentation of it?'

'There was some rubbish to put away. I've got the waste transfer note. But like I say, there was no asbestos.'

'Thank you,' said Ross. 'I'll not use this if I don't have to.'

He was about to leave, but took a copy of the waste transfer note first. Sitting back in the car, he thought about what had just happened. When the man talked about people in Glasgow giving him the job, Ross knew it would be a criminal element. All criminal elements needed normal work done as well. Depending on what you were doing, sometimes they paid a good rate. And there were people who were not criminals who supplied this work. Sometimes it was difficult not to. You could be coerced into it.

Ross didn't have any beef with the company he was sitting

at now, but he wondered how the headmistress got involved in that. There were also forms up there on the schoolbooks. There were finances run through. He had seen where money had been paid. And no doubt it was paid legitimately. But for what? And then the equipment had been taken out and put into vans and had gone into town.

Having made good progress at his first stop-off, Ross was then driving across to the east side of the city to another industrial estate. This one was more modern, and the factory he entered was clean and crisp. He'd never seen bag manufacturing before, and entered the front office quite optimistic. The secretary smiled at him. 'Hello, I'm DS Alan Ross. I'd like to speak to your manager.'

'He's inside his office. Just a second.'

Twenty seconds later, a man bounded out. He was broad and had a big jovial smile on his face. 'Hello, I understand you're with the police.'

'Detective Sergeant Alan Ross. I'd just like to speak to you about the bags you produce.'

'Of course. Come through to the office.'

Ross was taken through. He sat down and a cup of coffee was brought in to him. Around the office were pictures that looked like sponsorship and a growing factory. Ribbons being cut. Plaques being held up. Cheques at charity events.

'You've done well then,' said Ross.

'We're doing very well. Not been in production that long. Five years.'

'I want to talk about the bags you produce, specifically for Apple Cross Academy.'

'I don't recognise the account.'

'Maybe we can look at the supplier you give them to. I think

171

it's Perkins.'

'Oh, we do a lot of work with Perkins. We supply a lot of different schools, a good company to work with. Never had a problem with them.'

'Well, one of the bags you provide for them goes to Apple Cross Academy.'

'Just a moment,' said the man. He pressed a buzzer, and his secretary came in.

'Get Lorraine in, please,' he said. 'I think she might be the person we need.'

The secretary disappeared, and the manager explained.

'Lorraine is one of our sales reps. She'll know where the end product was for. Often we produce to a certain standard and then other companies will apply the print or something on the outside. So, a lot of our bags are completely the same. We provide certain standard levels of bags. But Lorraine will know where the end product's going. She arranges a lot of the sales.'

Lorraine was a forty-year-old woman with long black hair. She strode into the office, smiling at her boss, and then turned to Ross.

'Lorraine,' said her boss, 'I was just saying you'll be the person our detective here needs to talk to. This is DS Alan Ross. He's looking into bags that go to Applecross Academy.'

'Oh yes, Perkins, through the account.'

'What can you tell me about them?' asked Ross.

'Let's go have a look at them,' said Lorraine. 'It'll be the easiest way.'

Lorraine led the way out of the office, Ross in the middle with the boss following. His interest was clearly piqued that the police wanted to know about some of his products as they ended up in a large storeroom. Lorraine walked over to some large boxes.

'This is similar stock that we've got packed at the moment to be sent out.'

She pulled a large cardboard box off the shelf and Ross went to help her, but she shook her head. She placed the box on the floor, took out a safety knife from her back pocket and cut open the box. From inside, she pulled out a bag, which was wrapped in plastic. On opening it, she presented it to Ross.

'These are the bags we send them. They're standard bags, as you can see, enough to go away on trips. I think that's what they said. There are places for the shoes, there are places for everything. We send them two types of bag; this is one of them.'

'Two types,' said Ross. 'How do you mean?'

'Well, we have a special type of bag as well.'

'Special,' said Ross.

'Yes. There's a second compartment in the other one.'

'Can I see it?' asked Ross.

'Of course. Hang on a minute.'

Lorraine looked along the shelf, pulled out another box and cut it open. Clearly there were some staff not quite happy that a salesperson was ripping into the stock. But they stayed at a distance, aware that the boss was with her.

'Here's the other one,' she said, unpacking it and presenting it to Ross.

'It's exactly the same,' said Ross.

'No, it's not. Look in here.' Lorraine opened up the bag, and Ross couldn't see anything inside untoward.

'Put your hand in here, feel along, go underneath this piece of material, and if you pull this back, that zip opens up to a compartment. Thin, but a secret one in here. It's just a way of protecting goods.'

'Why does the school want it?'

'Like I say, they didn't want them all like that. These ones are slightly more expensive because of the added extra in the middle, although the other one is very similar. You just can't access that middle bit. There's a small amount of filler in it.'

'Do you know what quantity they order these in?'

'Well, they get an intake of, what, about one hundred a year, don't they?'

'And how much do they order of one and of the other?'

'Just a second,' she said. The woman went over to a station and typed into a computer. She came back two minutes later. 'It's about a three-to-one ratio in favour of the bags without the secret compartment.'

'Three to one? That's interesting,' said Ross.

'Why?' asked Lorraine.

'Afraid I can't say,' said Ross. 'But thank you. That's interesting. Very interesting.'

Chapter 21

Macleod sat in the car as Susan Cunningham drove them down into Applecross and to the flat of Keira Saunders. There was a driving wind as they approached, and as they got out of the car, Susan glanced across the road. The little old lady Annie was watching from the window. She gave a wave. Susan gave a slight nod back and then looked towards Keira's flat. There was nobody at the window. Approaching the door that led through to all four flats in the building, Macleod pressed the buzzer showing Keira's flat.

'Hello?'

'Hello, I'm Detective Chief Inspector Seoras Macleod. I'm here with DC Susan Cunningham, whom you've met before. I'd like to come in and have a word with you.'

'Okay, oh, right; just give me a moment.'

Macleod waited, and two minutes later the door was buzzed. They took the brief steps up to Keira's flat, where she was at the door. The woman was wrapped in a large dressing gown.

'Forgive me,' she said, 'just got out of the shower.' Macleod stared. Her hair was slightly wet at the top, but it wasn't wet at the bottom, not like you'd be in the shower. Her skin also didn't look wet. Instead, he simply nodded and asked if they could come in.

'Of course,' she said, and took them through to her small sitting room where Macleod looked around. There weren't many pictures there, as had been previously noted by Perry.

'We've received some information that you received several male visitors after you moved here. One was Max, your partner. My condolences on your loss.'

'That's right,' said Keira. 'Thank you. Yes, Max used to come, of course.'

'Donnie from the school, the janitor. He comes as well, does he?'

'Yes,' said Keira. 'Donnie's a poor soul, but he's very kind. Some of the girls tease him, but he doesn't deserve to be teased. He's lovely. Most of them actually like him.'

'Has he ever been inappropriate with you?' asked Macleod.

'In what way?'

'Went to touch you? Said something inappropriate? Talked about your body? Even made a rude comment about being pregnant. Anything like that?'

'I'm not sure Donnie knows how to be rude. Or how to be inappropriate?'

'Why did you say that?' asked Macleod.

'Well, I was once here when he called, and he was dropping stuff off. I answered in just a towel at the door, and he walked on in. He didn't ask if he could come in; he just walked on in and sat down. But he never looked at me, you know. I disappeared to get changed and came back out. And Donnie said nothing. It was almost as if, well, Donnie didn't know to look. Most guys would have looked, you know.'

'So what does he do when he's here?' asked Susan.

'He brings me flowers and food. It's lovely, he brings me flowers to cheer me up. Asks nothing in return, never looks for anything. In fact the only thing he looks for is if I smile when he gives me the flowers. He wants to know that they, well . . . they bring me a bit of happiness. He says I've had it difficult. Donnie's referring to Max a lot when he says that.'

'And he's never said anything inappropriate, never tried to make any sort of advance on you,' re-iterated Macleod.

'I told you, Donnie wouldn't know how to make an advance on a woman. I'm not even sure Donnie knows where to look. I've seen a lot of guys in my time, and Max, well, Max knew where to look, and what he wanted. I mean, it's fine, cos I wanted it too. But Donnie, the whole idea of sex and all of that, I don't think it's even in Donnie's head. I don't think Donnie knows. I'm not even sure if he knows how men and women produce children.'

'What about your other visitor?' asked Macleod. 'James, the PE instructor from the academy.'

'Yes, he's been coming here. He's sent by the school to make sure I'm okay.'

'You heard that he's died?' asked Macleod.

Keira nodded and went quiet for a moment.

'Why him?' asked Susan.

'How do you mean?' asked Keira.

'Why James? Why not send one of the female teachers? You're pregnant. You're away from home. I mean, some of those teachers might help you. Advise you from a woman's perspective.'

'I don't know how many of them even had kids. James was better with the DIY and that. He could do things around the flat. Since Max died, I have got no one to do that sort of thing.'

'But they sent him from the start, as soon as you got moved down here,' said Susan.

'Lot to do at the start. Lot to get sorted.'

'You seem to do okay though,' said Macleod. The room did indeed have some excellent furniture. There was a television, there was stereo, there was everything you could want. And yet Macleod also thought more than Kiera could afford, a pregnant woman with no money.

'School has been very generous. And some of the local people too.'

'So I hear,' said Macleod. 'You seem to receive a lot of parcels.'

'I'm sorry?'

'You usually receive a lot of parcels,' said Susan. 'We know because the postman and other delivery drivers have said your flat is a frequent stop-off point on their rounds.'

'You know, people are just generous. But they're usually items for the house, for, you know, food.'

'I can certainly see that. Can I ask you something else? And I hope I don't sound too rude,' said Macleod. 'There're no photographs of Max here.'

'No, there's not,' said Kiera. 'Too hard. Too much to bear. Max's death was hard to take.'

'Of course,' said Macleod. 'I can appreciate that. It's not unusual after the death of a loved one for people to struggle to even see them. Other people go the other way, of course. They want to have mementos of them everywhere. We're all different.'

However, he was unconvinced and stood up. A telltale sign, Susan noted. He walked over to the window and looked out of it. There, looking back from the other side of the road, was Annie at her window. Macleod thought for a moment.

'I'm going to ask something of a more personal nature,' said Macleod. 'I hope it won't upset you. It's about Max.'

'Okay,' said Kiera.

'Max had an identifying tattoo. Just around the pelvic area, a little up from his scrotum. It was a gang tattoo, at least that's what we're identifying it as. I assume you probably saw it, given the position it was in, if the two of you were intimate. And I was just wondering if you knew what gang it was from, if you had any idea. I mean, it's a pretty obvious tattoo, even if it was a strange place to put it.'

'Yes, yes, it is strange, isn't it?'

'Did you have any idea of what it meant?'

'No,' she said.

'Any idea? Any idea what the lion was for?'

'No.'

'Any idea of what the letters V, D, and T stand for?'

'None,' said Kiera.

'You never thought to ask him about it.'

'Not really. It wasn't what we were there for. And after I got pregnant, we didn't get it on. Well, he left me alone, so to speak.'

'Okay,' said Macleod. 'That can happen. Some men don't think it's something that should be done. But you have no idea what the tattoo meant?'

'Absolutely none.'

Macleod looked out the window again, and Annie was still looking back.

'What about James? You'd have seen him a lot if he were coming down here on the Academy's behalf. He ever talk to you about any of his relationships or what was happening up at the school?'

'No. I mean, we didn't talk that much. He came in, he did what he had to do on the DIY front. He asked some basic questions. Was I all right for money? Was I all right for food? Things like that. And then he'd go.'

'How often was he here and for how long?' asked Macleod.

'Never more than about an hour.'

'Okay,' said Macleod. 'You clearly have been in the shower and you were wanting to get dressed. We'll get out of here. Thank you. You've been very helpful.'

Macleod turned and saw Susan stand up, looking at him with questioning eyes. Macleod stepped over and shook Kiera's hand. 'Pleasure meeting you. All the best with the delivery and that. How many months are you now?'

'I think we're seven. Six or seven.'

'Getting close then. All the best with it.'

He turned and left, Susan in tow, and heard the door close behind him. Susan went to speak, but Macleod put his hand up quickly.

'In the car,' he said. They walked away. Heading back towards the car, Macleod knew that Keira was watching them from the window. Only when inside the car did Macleod speak.

'Go on then,' he said. 'You're dying to ask.'

'What tattoo? Did you check? Have you been through the morgue notes without me knowing?'

'No,' said Macleod. 'Just a hunch I had. The tattoo doesn't exist. Well, at least as far as I know.'

'You played her.'

'Yes. I wanted to know about her and Max. I wanted to know if that child is his. Possibilities. She could have been having a relationship with Max and probably was. Or, has he

180

been dragged into it as an alibi?'

'In what way?'

'Was the kid set up? Was Max duped? Get him in a situation, get him drunk, get him drunk so he doesn't remember. Tell him they did it. Tell him it's his kid.'

'What about when the kid pops out? If the kid looks different.'

'Who's going to ask that?' said Macleod. 'Really? Who's going to ask that? Unless the kid comes out black and he is a white father. Or they come out Asian when it's meant to be somebody from the Mediterranean. There has to be a significant difference. Clearly, black child meant to come from a white mum and a white father doesn't work. But we have got nobody of a different ethnicity here involved with Kiera.

'So I asked about a tattoo. If she hadn't seen it since the tattoo doesn't exist, she would have turned around and said, I never saw one down there. If that was the case, if she'd seen him as she said, she would have cried foul. As she hasn't seen him in that state, the likelihood of him having had sex with her is next to zero. I think he's been duped. I think the likelihood is they got him drunk somehow.'

'So, you think it's one of the others?' asked Susan.

'It's not Donnie. Perry, Ross, now myself, the rest of us believe it's not Donnie. Donnie just doesn't have the capacity. She said that herself.'

'She could be lying, though.'

'Why? Donnie's got a job.'

'She might not want to live with Donnie. She might not want Donnie.'

'Susan, you've seen Donnie. If you didn't want Donnie near you, would you just say no?'

'Of course,' said Susan.

'And it would work. People would understand. You could turn around and say, this guy's bothering me. Get him away. And people would react. Now, if it were somebody nicer, they might not react the same. They might think you're overplaying it. It's people's bias. They can make people like Donnie into sex pests when he doesn't have any notion, particularly about sex.'

'James then?'

'James,' said Macleod. 'He's down here straight away. Oh, he has to come because of the DIY. As an academy, you'd be sitting saying, let's get a female down. She's a pregnant teenage girl in a place of her own. It's got to be a woman, or at least a woman and a man. He's popping in for over an hour at a time. Even if you're down doing DIY works, you're going to have somebody with you. And we hear from Annie across the road that he's actually in there for longer than Keira said. It's James's. It's got to be. That must be James's kid.'

'Well, if it is, then who killed him?' asked Susan. 'Is Kiera a woman somebody hungered after? It doesn't get Donnie off the hook either. If Donnie's moral, if Donnie is not the threat, but Donnie thinks that somebody's done something to her, maybe Donnie would react.'

'There's too much going on,' said Macleod. 'Possibly things going on here that we're not seeing. There's something else. I can feel it. There's a thread that we haven't pulled out yet. Hopefully, Ross will have it pulled out. I think he's on to something. We'll see what Perry finds out from Donnie about the peepholes.'

Chapter 22

Perry ambled across to the lodge where Donnie stayed. He wasn't looking forward to this interview as he thought Donnie was innocent. Donnie was truly innocent. Innocent of mind, as well as of any crime. Perry was worried that he was being used as a scapegoat. And Donnie possibly wasn't clever enough to protect himself.

Perry's nature was to be kind to people like that. Protective. But he also was a detective, so he couldn't assume. This meant that sometimes he'd have to ask questions that really were uncomfortable. Ones that shouldn't be asked of an innocent man. Of course, until proven innocent, the questions had to be asked.

Perry knocked on the door and was soon received by Donnie.

'Come in. Do you want coffee?'

'Yes,' said Perry. 'I'll take a coffee. I take it you've opened up?'

'I've been all round and opened up. Of course, I'm not opening up certain places,' said Donnie. 'Your police people have lots of different places now.'

'Terrible about James,' said Perry.

'I don't understand,' said Donnie. 'Why kill him? Why do

that to someone? And why then put a doll with him?'

'You mean the mannequin?'

Donnie looked at him, eyes blank.

'It's just another word for doll,' said Perry.

Donnie made the coffee, handed one to Perry, and they sat down in Donnie's small living room. Everything was quite simple, really. There was a picture of what Perry presumed was Donnie's extended family. There was a football calendar on the wall, and Donnie had circled when particular matches were on.

'You like football then?'

'My dad likes football. I always ring him on those days to ask how the match went.'

'That's very nice of you,' said Perry.

'My dad says you should help people. He says you should try to be good with them.'

'My colleague said that you visit one of the girls in town, the one who got pregnant.'

'She's going to have a baby,' said Donnie. 'She needs help. She smiles when I give her flowers, so I always take her flowers. But I get food for her too, because she doesn't have much. We're meant to give to those who don't have much.'

'Indeed,' said Perry. 'I need to talk to you about something now. I don't know if you're aware, but all the senior staff have had someone make a peephole into their dwellings, their accommodations.'

'Make a what?' asked Donnie.

'Somebody has gone up on the roofs and has drilled a hole through so that you can see. In the ladies' accommodation, it's been a hole through to their bathrooms, right above their bath. In James's, it was into his living room. They then covered the holes with little plastic caps.'

Donnie stood up suddenly. 'Why?'

'I'm sorry?' said Perry.

'Why? Why do you drill a hole into people's rooms? Why would you look in the bathroom? You poo. You wash. Why would you look in the bathroom?'

'I don't know,' said Perry.

'Who wants to see someone on the toilet? Why in the bath? And why would anyone want to see James in his living room? If you want to see people, just go to the door. Knock it.'

'I think they want to watch them without people knowing.'

'Why?' asked Donnie. There was a knock at the door. Perry watched as Donnie walked over to it. He opened the door, and two of the older schoolgirls were standing there. There was an exchange about the handle on one dorm being broken. Donnie said he would come and fix it as soon as he could.

From Perry's position, he saw the two young women and thought they were lovely in their own way. Donnie never seemed to appreciate anything of them. It was almost as if he didn't see them in that way.

Even on first glance, as much as Perry behaved completely appropriately, there was always that first look. The first glance where beauty is picked up by your mind, that natural instinct to pick the best mate, a drive that sends you looking. That seemed to be missing with Donnie. Far from being someone who would take inappropriate action with the schoolgirls, Donnie seemed to be somebody who was oblivious to the fact that they were developing into women. He didn't fit the image of a jealous killer.

When Donnie had closed the door and sat down again, Perry asked him about the buildings that were cleared out.

'I told your detective sergeant. I said to him, the company came up to do it, the Buchan Co. It wasn't done by me. I wasn't allowed.'

'And how did they do it? It was overnight, wasn't it?'

'They did it at night. Someone said it was to keep the noise to a minimum, to keep everybody out of the way when the asbestos was removed. I can't remove asbestos. I don't know how, and I don't have the training. Pretty sure they could have given me training.'

Perry wasn't so sure that they could. But that wasn't what he was interested in.

'What did the company do during the day?'

'Well, I think some of them went home,' said Donnie. 'You see, there were two different bits of the company.'

'Two different bits?'

'Yes, there was the company who went home. The man in charge went home, then came back. He was angry. At the end, he was angry. I remember speaking to the headmistress, and she said the man had been angry.'

'What over?' asked Perry.

'Didn't say to Donnie. Something to do with the job.'

'What was the other bit of the company?'

'When they came, there was the van with Buchan Co. on it. But there are another couple of vans, and they seemed to put most of the things into them. I could only see from a distance, but these vans got full. I heard they went into town and stayed in town.

'During the day, they stayed in town. They worked through the night,' said Donnie. 'So, during the day, I think they slept.'

'How do you know?'

'Because I visited Keira. I was visiting Keira, and I saw the van in town. It was next to the old Hughes residence. So, they must have had a B&B. They found a B&B in town and went to bed. That's what it must have been. The old Hughes residence is all boarded up. So it can't have been that.'

'So, let me understand this correctly, Donnie. You're saying that when they came to do the job, there was one van with Buchan and Co. on it. That was the boss man, yes?'

'Yes,' said Donnie. 'But he didn't stay in town; he didn't stay; he went back to Glasgow, I think, or whatever his home is. The people in that van didn't stay. The other van, which they loaded stuff into, stayed in town. During the day, it was in town because it was there when I visited Kiera.'

'What's the old Hughes residence?' asked Perry.

'Hughes used to be quite a big family; they had quite an extensive building there, but it fell into disrepair and ruin. Nobody goes into it now.'

'Okay,' said Perry. 'Interesting.' He asked Donnie to come with him. 'I want you to look at one of the peepholes, Donnie, if that's okay.'

When they got there, Donnie looked at the hole and turned to Perry. 'This has been cut wrong. You can cut this better. Much cleaner, easier way to do it, and you can make a little cover. This rubber would move so that you could kick it off. Instead, you could screw down a proper cover, make a flap. It would be much better if you could also put a tube in, maybe a bit of glass. You'd see a hole in the ceiling unless you can get glass you can look through and not from the other side; that could work.'

'It's right above the bath there. I mean if Miss Waters was in there you'd see everything.' Perry watched Donnie's reaction. There wasn't even a flinch out of him.

'I don't see the point in that. Maybe if they had the football on or maybe one of the pay channels for football or films,' said Donnie. 'Maybe one of the girls would like to watch it. Why would they want to watch someone in the bath? The one in the living room makes more sense, doesn't it?'

'I guess it does, Donnie,' said Perry. He walked with Donnie, pointing out where the other holes had been.

'You'd need keys to get in, though, wouldn't you?'

'Keys?' said Donnie. 'Why?'

'Because you'd have to go in without the person's permission.'

'They didn't ask for them to be there?' queried Donnie.

'Well, no,' said Perry. 'Why would you want someone to put a peephole into your bathroom?'

'I don't know,' said Donnie. 'I just thought that they wouldn't—'

He seemed to clam up for a moment and then he reacted.

'You can't do that. You can't put something in somebody's house without asking them. Get the key and get into their house, but only if you have told them what you're doing and why you're doing it. That's how it works. You tell them and they know what you've done. Then they come back, they look at it and if there's something wrong, they tell you—I don't like this, I like that—you sort it out. But you can't sort it out if you don't have their permission. You need their permission to go in. The headmistress told me that. Never go in without being told to do something. And then we have the key. They trust me with the key because I don't do that. I don't go in unless I'm told.'

'Thank you, Donnie,' said Perry. He walked back with the man to Donnie's lodge. 'What are you going to do now?' asked

Perry.

'I have a handle to fix. The ladies who came earlier said their room handle is broken. I need to fix it.'

Perry watched Donnie disappear into his workroom, take out some work gear and a new handle, and march off. He gave Perry a smile as he walked past. Perry wondered what was going on. *Was Donnie just expendable? Is that why somebody was trying to fit Donnie up? What was going on behind the scenes in this school?*

Donnie was a simple soul. He probably couldn't argue his way out of anything. He did have access, though. Access to the school. He was a janitor. He had basic skills, but he had such an attitude about how that hole was made. Almost inferior. There was no pride in the work. He felt Donnie would have taken pride in whatever he did. But his idea of the cover. Maybe his cover would be better. You wouldn't be able to find it.

Perry shook his head. Donnie was all wrong for this. He never flinched at those girls. Perry thought that if he took Donnie to a gentleman's club, the man would wonder why he was there. And weren't the women getting cold?

For a moment, Perry chortled. And then he grimaced. Donnie might not be the right person, but they needed to find out who it was before someone tried to pin it on Donnie. That annoyed Perry. It was one thing to murder people; it truly was, and not a good thing—but to pin it on an innocent like this. Perry's back was up; he knew it. They'd have to find this killer and find him soon, before more innocent people suffered.

Chapter 23

'And still they want another press conference,' said Macleod.

'It's part of the job, though, isn't it?'

'It's part of Hope's job. If Hope were here, Hope would do this.'

'You're not comfortable with the press, are you?' said Susan.

'I'm not comfortable with the whole thing, if I'm honest. A girls' school. How did I end up having to deal with a girls' school when Hope went off on maternity leave? It wouldn't be done, you know. No, girls' schools were girls' schools back in my day. The idea of a male PE teacher as well.'

'I'm not sure they would do that in a state school, although state schools are mixed, aren't they?' said Susan.

'Anyway. Let's get this press conference done. They'll be desperate for answers,' said Macleod. 'But the usual thing, constant questions. "Are you doing enough? Are you this?"' He could feel his phone vibrating in his pocket. 'Oh, hang on a minute,' he said, taking out the phone to see it was Ross calling.

'I hope you've had a good morning.'

'Excellent one, sir,' said Ross. 'I've been to Buchan and Co. Been interesting. They said there was no asbestos in the buildings. But we've got an asbestos note on the school records.'

'So why didn't they tell anyone?' asked Macleod.

'Apparently, they were sent there by, well, I think it's a criminal element. Buchan and Co. seem to be people who get pulled in to do legitimate jobs for them. So, he didn't really want to say no. A bit scared. Was told basically that once he realised there was no asbestos there, they were just to ignore it. Now, the company has done nothing illegal. They didn't sign the asbestos removal chitty, but it looks like Georgie Mackie did.'

'So what? What were they doing there?'

'There was equipment that had to be taken out,' said Ross. 'I think Buchan and Co. were there because they needed someone who could do that, and do it properly. They would leave behind a sensible looking interior. Also with such a company being there, people would have thought it was a pretty normal operation.'

'But they took everything out at night, didn't they?' said Macleod.

'So, what they were taking out, obviously, was the important bit. The guy from Buchan said it was just equipment. He recognised little of it.'

'But what did he do with it?'

'Well, this is the thing. He's got a waste note. But the waste note is so small for the size of the buildings. He said there were other vans there that weren't part of his company.'

'What do you mean there were other vans?'

'Well, he thought they were from the school,' said Ross. 'Anyway, they seemed to take away the equipment. Buchan, I believe, was there not for the asbestos, but to do the decommissioning of the equipment and take it out. He also would have been a legitimate bill. So, on record, it would look like something was legitimately done.'

'However, the equipment, whatever it is, has been moved somewhere else.'

'I think so. That's what it seems to me. I also went to look at the bag company,' said Ross.

'What did that throw up?' asked Macleod.

'I think the bags are being used to carry something. Maybe drugs? Something like that? There is a three-to-one ratio of bags being sent. Three bags are normal bags. The other bag is a special bag. It's got a special compartment in it. There's nothing illegal in the production of the bags, but they're being used, I think, to move gear that's illegal. But listen to this. The bags are being bought in a three to one ratio. Three normal to one special. Well, we have four houses in the school. One of the houses, Madson, is always on its trips when the drug shipments occur into the cities. So, maybe that's the house that gets the special bags.'

'Get back here, okay? I'm going to talk to Perry. Good work, Ross. I think there's definitely something going on. I believe there's another enterprise at work here. These murders, and the idea that they're to do with some sort of love triangle or sexual intent, are just a cover.'

'On my way,' said Ross. 'Quick as I can.'

'Press conference then,' said Susan.

'Hang on,' said Macleod, and called Perry on the phone.

'Where are you?' asked Macleod as Perry answered.

'I'm still here at the school, not long finished with Donnie.'

'Things are coming to a head,' said Macleod, and relayed all that Ross had said. 'We need to be careful, Perry. We need to move, but we can't spook anyone.'

'Listen,' said Perry, 'talking to Donnie this morning—the contractors stayed in town. He said Buchan went home, but this other van that you've talked about, these other people, well, he said that they stayed in town. Donnie confirmed that there were other people. They weren't from the school, though.'

'Did Donnie say where the contractors were staying?' asked Macleod.

'Yes, it's beside the old Hughes residence. There's a B&B down that way.'

'Get down there,' said Macleod. 'Get down there and check. See where they stayed.'

'What are you going to do?' asked Perry.

'I've got to hold a press conference right now. I don't want not to do it, in case people think something is up. So, you go down and check this out, Perry. Get the answer back to me.'

'Will do,' said Perry.

* * *

Having taken the call from Macleod, Perry drove into town. It wasn't difficult to find the old Hughes residence as it was an imposing building, and along from it there were indeed some B&Bs. The Hughes residence, however, was boarded up. Perry thought it didn't look the most attractive place to stay beside. However, he rapped the door of the B&B that was next to it.

'Hello,' said a man standing in his dressing gown.

'I believe you operate a B&B here, sir. My name's Detective Constable Warren Perry. I'd like to ask you for some information.' He quoted the date of the works up at the school, and the man looked back at him. 'I haven't been a B&B for at least six months. You're talking about next door; Agnes is the one you want.'

'Thank you, sir,' said Perry and moved next door. A woman, presumably Agnes, came to the door dressed in a long skirt and blouse. She gave a smile as Perry stood there.

'You looking for a B&B, love?'

'No,' said Perry, again presenting his credentials. 'I'm Detective Constable Warren Perry. I'm looking to see who stayed here back on this date.' Perry wrote the date down for her, and she turned, went back inside and then came to the door with a comprehensive book.

'Right,' she said, 'who did you say was staying here?'

'It would have been some contractors, mostly men.'

'Got a woman and a small child. That was it. Nobody else stayed here.'

'There was a van parked outside the Hughes residence. It was seen,' said Perry.

'Doesn't mean it's me. You sure it wasn't anywhere else along here? Maybe it had to do with the Hughes building? I've seen people sometimes go in there.'

'Really?' said Perry.

'Quietly, round the back.'

'Okay,' said Perry and thanked the woman.

He walked back to the Hughes residence. The windows were indeed boarded up, as was the front door, so Perry took a walk around the back of it. There was a door at the rear that wasn't boarded, but it was padlocked. Perry came up close to it, and he could hear a low hum from inside. *Was electricity running?*

It seemed strange. Maybe it was dehumidifiers. Abandoned houses often were damp, and they kept the air flowing. Maybe that was why someone went in and out. Perry returned around to Agnes again, asking who owned the building. She said it was the Hughes family, but a local agent now had the key. They'd been called before to enter the building to deal with rats, although that was some time ago. Agnes had the number.

Perry called the agent on the phone.

'McCann's. How can I help you?'

'I'm standing outside the old Hughes residence. My name's Detective Constable Warren Perry. There's a hum going on inside the building. I'm interested in finding out what the current state of the property is. I was advised by a nearby B&B owner that you had the keys for the property and were looking after it for the Hughes family.'

'Well, that's correct. We used to call by once a week, but we received a communique since then that we weren't to do that. So, yes, we do still hold a key, but we haven't been in that building for a good four or five months.'

'Okay,' said Perry. 'There's a padlock on the back door. Would you be able to come round and let me in to see inside the building? I need to satisfy myself that hum is coming from something sensible. Did you have dehumidifiers in the building at all?'

'We never put any in, but we still have the keys and right of access. So, by all means, officer, if you hang on, I'll be round in about ten minutes.'

Ten minutes later, a man in a suit appeared, and Perry presented his credentials to him.

'Okay, Constable Perry, we'll let you in then round the back. Let's go.' The man walked around with Perry, opened the lock and went to go inside.

'If you just stay here, sir, I'll go in first, just in case there's anything untoward.'

Perry pulled a pocket torch out from inside his jacket and shone it into the darkness inside. With the windows boarded up, there was no light in the hallway. However, as Perry walked along, he was surprised to see that there was a light coming from upstairs.

Perry, however, first pushed open the door on his right-hand side, which went through to an enormous room that took up most of the bottom floor of the property. Here was a myriad of different equipment. He looked at it. Some of it looked scientific. He recognised that some of it was potentially drug-making equipment.

Perry skirted right out of the room, up the stairs to where he'd seen the light. As he reached the top, he opened a door that led into a room that was filled with plants. The plants were on benches, and there were large heaters. There were temperature controls dotted here and there. It didn't look as if it had been installed properly, more of a temporary thing. And it was certainly not a room that was on the scale of downstairs. This was quite small. Perry picked up his phone and called Jona.

'Jona,' he said.

'Perry, don't tell me I'm coming all the way back down. I'm up in Inverness now.'

'I'm going to show you a video. I want you to tell me what I'm looking at.' He set his phone up and began to swing its camera around the room.

'Cannabis, Perry, it's fairly small scale.'

'Fine,' said Perry, 'now hang on. I'm going to go elsewhere in this building, and I want you to tell me what I'm looking at.'

Perry went back down to the larger room downstairs. He took his time walking around, allowing Jona to look at the different equipment that was in the room.

'Perry,' said Jona. 'This is drug-making equipment. This is serious drug-making equipment. Upstairs, that's cannabis. It's not worth much on the street. Yes, you'll make a bit, but with this equipment here, you'll make a lot with it. An awful lot. Are there any drugs about?'

'Not that I can see,' said Perry.

'I'm coming down,' she said. 'Close off the building. Lock it. Get someone to cordon it off. Tell me you have touched none of it.'

'I'm not an idiot,' said Perry.

'I'll be down. You'd better tell Macleod.'

Perry said that he would and then walked to meet the estate agent outside. 'I'm afraid I've found items in here that may be of a criminal nature. I'm going to ask for the key from you.'

'I understand,' said the man. 'Obviously, I'm happy to comply. Just for the record, I have no idea what was in there. Last time I was inside, there was nothing.'

'Duly noted,' said Perry. 'We're just going to hold here until I can get some police officers to come and protect the building. If you just remain here with me, they'll be able to take a statement from you about your dealings with the building in the last while. There's no need for an alarm, sir. I just need to know when things were transferred over.'

Perry walked around to the front of the building after asking the agent to remain at the back. As he got to the front and picked up his phone, he called the local station, asking them to send some men down from the school to assist him. He then went to place a call through to Macleod.

As he did so, he saw Mia Xien walking past. She was staring right at him. She looked anxious. In fact, she looked more

197

than anxious. And her pace quickened, and suddenly she was in a car. He went to walk over to her, but she drove off quickly, far too quickly.

Chapter 24

acleod was cutting a stonewall figure, and Susan thought he should warm up a bit. The way to deal with the press, according to Hope, was to be convivial. Firm at times, yes, but be convivial. Make it look as if you're giving them information, even if you were telling them nothing. Macleod wasn't even bothering.

She watched as he was asked a question, to which he said absolutely nothing, while rambling on for about three sentences. She also saw him reach down towards his trouser pocket. His phone must have been vibrating; she was sure of it. That's where he kept it. A moment later, her own phone vibrated. She picked it up. It was Perry.

'Where's the boss?' he asked.

'He's in the middle of the press conference. What's up, Perry?' she asked.

'I've just been down to the old Hughes residence. We've got a cannabis factory upstairs. Downstairs, we've got enough drug equipment to make street-sold drugs and proper money off it. I checked with Jona, and she said it was the real deal. I think they used to run it up in the school. For whatever reason, they've brought it down here now. The agent for the house says he was told not to go into the place and hasn't been in for the last five months. I heard an electrical hum, which is why I got in.'

'Wow. That puts a completely different light on it. So, Ross is right about the bags then. We think they're shipping drugs out with the girls. This is crazy.'

'More than that, I've just seen Mia Xien. And she has just seen me outside the building. Susan, she took off like a bullet. Something's up. That woman knew what was in there. She knew what was going on. And she was panicking that I'm here.'

Susan watched Macleod continue to speak, but in the corner, the deputy headmistress was also watching him. At least she was until suddenly she reached for her own phone. The woman took a call while Susan was talking to Perry. Then Lily Waters and Pauline Drummond were suddenly summoned to her. They disappeared just as quickly.

Susan stalked around to the back of the platform that Macleod was speaking from, approached him from behind and tapped him on the shoulder. He was still in mid-speech and gave his head a little shake to show he didn't want her to interrupt him. However, Susan grabbed his shoulder and whispered in his ear, 'Now, it's important.'

'If you'll just excuse me a moment, I have to take an important call.' Macleod stood up and walked off the stage into the wings of the room where the press couldn't see him.

'Don't do that,' said Macleod. 'They'll think something's up. They'll be desperate to know what's going on. You never interrupt at a press conference unless it's life and death.'

'I think it might be,' said Susan. 'Perry's been down to the old Hughes residence. Contractors never stayed at the B&B.

Instead, the equipment that was in the outbuildings has gone into the old Hughes residence. Jona has seen the equipment. She says it's proper equipment for making high-value drugs.'

'Really,' said Macleod.

'It looks like Ross is right,' said Susan. 'The idea of the bags, the idea of shipping drugs down.'

'Right, I'll go in and finish the conference. We'll not say anything about it. And then—'

'Wait,' said Susan. 'Perry was outside the building waiting for police colleagues to come down and close it off. Mia Xien walks past him. He said she looked at him like she knew what was in there. She looked panicked. She got in her car. I've just seen the deputy headmistress take a call. Pauline Drummond, Lily Waters came to her, and then they went like a rocket.'

Susan saw Macleod's face suddenly darken. 'The car. Susan, get the car!'

'Are you going to close off the press conference?'

'No, the car. Just get the car. We've got to get to Keira's right now.'

Susan ran for the car, and Macleod left the building behind her, fumbling with his phone and trying to dial a number. As he approached the car, Susan could hear him talking to Perry.

'Keira Saunders's house, Perry. Go! Get there! She's under threat! Now!'

* * *

Perry closed the call as soon as Macleod said it. The mobile phone was dropped into his pocket, and he ran for the car. Keira Saunders's flat was not that far away, but Mia Xien had a head start on him. Applecross was not big, and Perry arrived at the flat within two minutes. He jumped out of the car and raced towards the main outside door which was open. Bolting through the door, he took the stairs up towards the upper-floor flat, and he could hear a hysterical Keira.

'I won't say. I won't.'

'You threatened before. You threatened to expose us for having this. We can't take chances. We can't take chances with you. You shouldn't have turned tail. You shouldn't have threatened.'

'Police!' shouted Perry. 'Police, now calm down, everyone.' But as Perry turned the corner to look inside Keira's flat, she saw Mia Xien with her hands around Keira's throat. She was throttling the woman.

'Put her down,' yelled Perry.

Mia turned to Perry, producing a small flick knife and left Kiera behind her. As she walked slowly towards Perry, with a menacing look in her eye, Kiera jumped Mia from behind. She was seven months, or thereabouts, pregnant, and the jump was awkward. She did, however, cling around Mia's neck, but the woman shrugged her off, dropping Kiera behind her. Perry took his chance.

Before Mia could react, Perry had charged. He dropped the right shoulder and hit her with all the practice of a Sunday afternoon rugby player. It wasn't the best connection, but it knocked the woman to the ground. He'd winded her too, for he could hear her struggling for breath.

Keira was rolling around behind them, unable to assist, and Perry tried to keep Mia on the ground. The knife was out of her hand, and Perry forced one hand down and then caught the other. He was on top of Mia, and his considerable bulk was pinning her down hard. Perry had her subdued. He just had to work out how to get the cuffs from his back pocket onto her arms and how to flip her over. But she was strong. Very strong. He'd have to be careful.

As he forced Mia's arms down to the ground, Perry grunted. It was taking a lot of effort. He pushed her wrists together slowly, grabbing them then with one hand, quickly reaching back to take the cuffs. It was then that he felt a blow to the back of the head. Perry collapsed.

* * *

'Go, Susan,' shouted Macleod in the car.

'I'm going!'

The car hurtled around the corner, and Susan slammed on the brakes, pulling up in front of the flat.

'That's Perry's car,' cried Macleod, and jumped out of the vehicle. Susan joined him, and together they raced for the flat. As they approached, they could see Lily Waters and Pauline Drummond dragging Perry out of the building. He looked unconscious.

Susan bolted, much quicker than Macleod, who followed her as best he could. Pauline Drummond looked up and pulled a knife from her jacket as Susan approached, but Susan was far too quick for her. The younger woman ducked the stabbing attempt, grabbed a wrist, and drove it up the woman's back, causing the knife to fall. Within a few seconds, she had a handcuff on that wrist and was grabbing the other one, kicking her in the back of the legs, driving the knees to the ground.

As she did so, Pauline Drummond dropped Perry and reached for Susan. But Susan Cunningham was quick. She grabbed Pauline's wrist as she came for her, once again pushed her down towards the ground, forcing the woman onto her front.

'Handcuffs, sir,' shouted Susan.

As Macleod arrived, dropping and placing his knees on the back of Pauline Drummond, he took his handcuffs out. Susan tore off into the building. Macleod could hear other cars, but he didn't look until he had the handcuffs secured on Pauline Drummond. Only then did he turn and see the early arrival of the press.

Those who had been quickest, who had raced after him, and who were probably telling everyone else where to go, were now exiting their cars, complete with cameras. Macleod raised a hand to them.

'Stay back! It's not safe!'

Cameras clicked as Macleod shouted it. And then Susan was crashing backwards, careering out through the front door. She stumbled over Lily Waters lying on the ground and cracked her head on the ground. She looked stunned, and Macleod looked up to see Mia Xien suddenly appear at the front door. Cameras were clicking, and the woman clocked the press. She looked at Macleod kneeling on the ground and turned back inside the building.

'Are you okay?' Macleod said to Susan.

'Yes, yes. A sore head, but yes. Be careful. She knows how to fight. She's strong.'

Macleod stood up and thought for a moment. If that woman could knock Susan Cunningham back out of the flat, he wouldn't stand a chance. There were police arriving now, and Macleod thought he might stay until they got to him. Then they would run into the flat—except she might not come out the front door.

He turned and ran around the side of the building, down a small alleyway into what was the backyard of the flats. There were gardens here and there was a rear door. He quickly ran up beside it.

Macleod could hear the commotion from the front, hear the sirens as more police vehicles arrived. Ahead of him, opposite the door, was an array of bins, three for each house: normal waste, organic waste, recycling—a myriad of colours. But to the side of them was a small alleyway and a route out. There was a small river down there. There were other gardens.

She could get away. She'd have to come out the front or the back, surely, for she was trapped. If she came out the back, he'd have to stop her. For a moment he thought about bracing himself, about throwing himself at her. But then he simply stood upright against the wall, right beside the door, making sure he was on the side without the hinges.

It was ten seconds later when the door swung open. Mia Xien rushed out, down a step, ready to take off through the small gap by the bins and out to the river. She'd have been gone except a foot was hanging there. A single foot which caught Mia's foot as it went past. Her back foot then clicked into her front foot, and she went sprawling straight into the bins.

Macleod rushed and pulled them down until the woman was rolling around underneath them, struggling to get up. It took her a good fifteen seconds to fight her way out, fifteen seconds that allowed Macleod to shout for backup. By the time Mia had stood up, two constables had come around the corner and had pounced on her.

She was taken down to the ground. Handcuffs were placed on her wrists behind her back. Happy that the woman was now secure with the two constables, Macleod raced in through the back door. The flat owners from downstairs were standing at their doors, shocked looks on their faces, but Macleod was scanning the hallway.

Nothing. Kiera wasn't here. He leapt up the steps as best he could, and there in her doorway, found her lying on the floor.

Macleod bent down. He put his ear to her mouth. He could feel the breath. She was alive, but there was blood running from her head. Clearly, she'd also been bounced off the walls because there was blood in other places. Macleod picked up his phone, dialling for an ambulance. He hoped he wasn't too late.

* * *

The ambulance arrived, and the paramedics raced to Keira. Macleod got clear to let them do their work and stepped outside into a blinding array of flashes. He saw Perry and Susan, both looking a little bewildered.

'Are we okay?'

'Constables have Mia and are heading for the station. It's not a big one, so they're going to head on into Glasgow, get one of the bigger stations. I've said we need to take the others there too.'

'Yes,' said Macleod. 'We also need to get back up to the academy. Miss Fotheringham-Smythe needs to be picked up as well. Iris Adams too. They're all in on it. The whole senior staff knew. The murders were fallout,' said Macleod.

'Fallout?' said Susan.

'There was no sex scandal, no love triangles. There was nothing, except Kiera being pregnant with James's child. And then she blackmailed him. That's why she's got so much stuff. That's why Mia ran for her because she could spill all the beans. The rest of them were all still involved. But Kiera had a child to protect. She would grass for a safe place to bring up a child.'

Macleod grabbed hold of a local sergeant, and told him what he wanted. Half of the police at the flat made for the academy. There were plenty of uniforms around. He hoped they could grab everyone. He then turned to walk to the car, but in his face it felt like there were hundreds of microphones. It felt like he was on a catwalk with photographers everywhere.

'What's happened, Detective Chief Inspector? Have you apprehended the killer?'

Macleod stopped, looked around at them all. 'There will be a police conference in due time,' he said. 'At that, we will tell you what we can tell you. Until then, kindly give my colleagues room to do their jobs.'

With that, he simply walked on until he got into the car. The keys were still in it, and he made for the school. He left Perry and Susan to await paramedics, since both had suffered blows to the head. It was over. This was merely mopping up.

Chapter 25

'So, how's the little guy?'

Macleod was sitting in his office back in Inverness after several days of wrapping up the case. There would be paperwork to do, all the usual formalities, but it was done. He had been back home, and Jane had been delighted to see him. He'd found the contrast between being away and being home starker now than he ever had. She had, of course, teased him about his coming back to this older woman after being there amongst those teenage girls, but she was delighted to have him.

He would have to pop back down to Glasgow because the Glasgow Drugs Division was now heavily involved in the case as well. There hadn't just been murder. There had been drugs being run, and Macleod would have his comments and statements to make about that.

He had thought about calling Hope from her office. After all, the window was better to look out. But he wasn't going back to the past. This was temporary cover he was doing, and in truth, it hadn't been like those years before. Nothing had since he moved up.

The Forseti case had shocked him. He'd been so close to

losing people. Maybe he'd lost his edge. He hadn't lost his mind. He hadn't lost the ability to read what was going on. It was his quick action, his quick piecing together of the situation that had saved Keira Saunders.

'The wee man's great. And I'm not too bad either, thanks for asking,' said Hope.

'I know you'd be all right. How's John taking to it?'

'Seoras, He's loving it. We're heading off for a wee holiday soon. Getting away, a retreat. Away from everything. Looking forward to that. Might come back after that. Sounds like you managed without me though.'

'Me? No,' said Macleod.

'Can I call you back?' asked Hope. 'I'm actually out and about, just about to go in and see someone.'

'Okay,' said Macleod. 'Speak to you later.'

He put down the phone and looked out of the window. The view was rubbish. There was a knock at the door.

'Come in,' he said, and heard the door open. He turned around to see Hope, pushing a small pram. It wasn't like the old-fashioned ones. In some ways, it was quite small. But she was beaming. The red hair wasn't up in a ponytail, splaying instead across her shoulders. And yes, part of her looked tired. There was no doubt the wee man had been keeping her up. But she looked good.

'Visiting someone then?'

'Yes,' she said. 'You!' She reached into the pram. 'He needs fed,' she said, and walked over to Macleod's spare sofa at the side of the office.

'Do you have a bottle?' asked Macleod.

'No, it's on mum,' she said, and sat down on the sofa.

'I'll leave then,' said Macleod.

'Don't be so old,' said Hope. She adjusted her top and tucked Ian John underneath it, sat back and let him feed.

'It's discreet,' said Hope. 'There's no need. Come and sit beside me,' she said.

Macleod made his way over, even though he felt uncomfortable.

'So, tell me about this case. Perry was giving me bits and pieces on the way up, but I thought your office was quieter.'

'You could have fed him wherever you wanted. You've got your own office down there.'

'I wanted to see how you were,' said Hope.

'I'm fine.'

'Somebody said something to me.'

'Really?'

'Really,' she said.

'Well, I managed a case without you. You know what happened at the school.'

'Yes,' said Hope. 'Perry told me that much.'

'Well, the deputy head went missing.'

'Missing?' said Hope.

'She legged it out of there after sending the other two down to despatch Keira Saunders. We caught her heading to Glasgow a week later, though. The Glasgow drug section is uncovering more and more links. There's shock amongst the normal girls and their parents, the girls who came from the other three houses.

'Madson girls, well, they were working on low-level drugs in Glasgow. And they got scholarships over and into the school. A brilliant drug ring was set up. And then they were supplying in large quantities on school visits. Bags that were put on the buses, stayed on the buses while they went off to do something.

But of course, the buses went elsewhere. Bags were lifted off, drugs taken out, bags given back. Very smooth.'

'So what actually happened with the murders?'

'Well, the thing was that James, the PE teacher, had got Keira Saunders pregnant, the girl they tried to kill at the end. She was a Madson girl. Keira blackmailed them, saying she'd tell everything if they didn't help her out.

'Rather than cause a fuss, especially with the other girls, they decided not to dispose of her, but just put her up in the house. They had plenty of money coming in from the drugs. They needed then to get the drug production shifted. The trouble was that the school hierarchy, as told to us by Pauline Drummond, where you had the headmistress and then the deputy head, was just a cover. Miss Fotheringham-Smythe, the deputy head, was actually the person in charge in terms of the drug running.

'Georgie Mackie was the face of the school, but she was also responsible for setting up the production to get the drugs into Glasgow, Inverness, etc. However, with the contacts she was making, she took an extra unauthorised cut. She shouldn't have, and so she had to be eliminated. Miss Fotheringham-Smythe decided that Georgie needed to go, and James would go too, because James was now a liability, having got one of the young girls pregnant.'

'Full on,' said Hope.

'Apparently, he was quite popular among the Madson house girls. So, they decided they would set up a sexual murder, and that they would blame it on Donnie. Donnie was truly innocent, had no idea what was going on, but was simple enough that they thought they could put it on him. They moved the equipment down, first of all, into the new building in Applecross. Attention would be on the school after the murders, and on the headmistress and James. But the drug production would have moved.

'However, some girls also set up a temporary cannabis production upstairs in the place that they were meant to be watching. That was the trouble. They really had made these girls into entrepreneurs, even if they'd done it illegally. But they hadn't thought about Ross. Over the years, I've had my complaints about him. I've thought of him as not being sergeant material. But he's very good with his computers. He made links where there weren't any. He made links I couldn't have seen by correlating things, finding connections and then working out what those connections really were.

'The bags for one. The fact new bags were given to the girls when they arrived seemed innocuous. Then Ross traced them and discovered that only a quarter of the girls got a certain type of bag, which had a compartment inside it. I wouldn't have sorted this one out without Ross, I don't think.

'Jona too. Jona was the one who led me to think there might be more than one person. You couldn't do this killing like this on your own. And that was their downfall. It was too elaborate. They wanted all the focus to be on this killer, who was obsessed with Georgie. They wanted the story to be about sex, to be about longing and lust. And not about money making.

'Kiera was their downfall too. James put a spanner in the works by getting her pregnant. But they were going to give her a place, for James would soon be gone. Maybe they would deal more with her then, make her part of the murders, for Donnie visited her too. Wasn't much to pay for a flat for her, at least for a while. They did, however, kill off her boyfriend, at least her supposed boyfriend.

'Supposed boyfriend?' asked Hope.

'Keira said that she'd never had sex with Max, the guy from the electricians. He'd been drunk with her a few times, drunk to the point of not remembering anything he did. So, she told him they'd got it on. They hadn't, of course, but he thought it was his kid. However, they got worried that in the long run he might get close to her. He might be a complication. They killed him. Hit and run. Made it look perfectly normal. And she didn't care.'

'Wow,' said Hope. 'I've missed quite a bit, haven't I?' She adjusted herself as she moved Ian John onto her other side. Macleod looked away temporarily.

'What about you then?' he said.

'I'm good, but I'm here to talk about you. I'm taking my family away on a little holiday. But somebody told me you're having reservations.'

'I'm not having reservations. It's not reservations about this job. It's time for me to go, Hope.'

'What?' she blurted.

'This time being away, I missed her. I miss Jane. She deserves time with me. I run around now, the knees feel sore. Everything feels not right. How long do you get, Hope? How long do you get to stay in good health? I don't want to be the guy who comes home and then ends up in a wheelchair or feeling ill most of the time and is simply looked after. Jane and I have got to live. We didn't get our thirties and forties together, or even our fifties. We need to live now. She came up, she came to the house, she's living in Inverness and half the time she doesn't see me because this lunatic before you is charging around. I'm a celebrity now. I don't want to be a celebrity. I don't want to be the guy they all look at.'

213

'Well, at least now you understand how I feel.'

'I do,' said Macleod. 'Only, at least with me, they said it was for my mind. With you, it was about your figure. That's worse. Not anymore, though. I can't doubt you any longer, and if truth be told, I don't. You're ready for this job. You can handle whoever comes in to replace me.

'But I need to go. When you come back, I'm going. I will miss you all. In as much as I have loved working with you all, I have loved working with you the most, Hope. But sometimes you've got to do what's right for your family. And Jane's my family.'

They sat in silence for several minutes until Hope took Ian John off the breast and started to wind him. Macleod reached over.

'Can I?' he said.

'Do you know what you're doing?' asked Hope.

'No,' said Macleod. 'But I'm just trying to make him burp, aren't I? Like I burp. Gently on the back. Hold him. Maybe bounce him a little. Gently on the back. Yes?'

Macleod tenderly took the baby and placed him on his shoulder. Carefully, he tapped Ian John on the back.

'Besides,' said Macleod, 'I'm not going away from your life. I'm godfather to this one. I'll be about. But you and I won't have to talk about dead people all the time. I've had my fill of evil motives, of seeing the bad side of humanity. I need to get out and see some good. I don't want to die a miserable sod.'

'Even though you've lived most of your life like that,' said Hope. Macleod shot her a look. 'You're not going to be my boss,' she said. 'I can say what I want.'

Macleod laughed, and suddenly Ian John burped. A bit of sick went over Macleod's shoulder and down the back of his shirt.

'Oh, sorry,' said Hope. She went over to the buggy and took out a cloth and started to rub Macleod's back. 'Thing is, Seoras,' she said, 'it doesn't smell. Not until they get on to proper food.'

'I also hate this view,' said Macleod. 'Don't let them take you away from the DI job. Don't move up too quickly. Be at the forefront. I'm away from everybody here. You don't get the cut and thrust of the office. The thrill of the chase still excites me, but my body can't do it. I need more time doing things like this.' Macleod continued to pat Ian John on the back.

'I think Jane's a bit old for kids. You're being optimistic there.'

'Not kids,' said Macleod, realising she was joking. 'I need to do things with Jane. We need to get away. We need to live. She has a lot of things she wants to do. That's why she's good for me. Me, I see work. I see everything that's bad to be put right. She sees the joy in life, and has fun with it. That's why we work together. Together, she complements me. And in doing so, she lifts me up. And she changes me.'

'We are in a deep mode today, aren't we?' said Hope.

'You never think like this?'

'I have been up through the night feeding this little one. I have been changing nappies, and so has John. Occasionally, when he goes to sleep, we look at each other and fall into bed, and don't do anything. In the past, we'd have loved a couple of hours to get each other into bed. Now, we don't even realise the other one's in bed; we go to sleep so quickly.'

She reached forward and took Ian John back off Macleod. 'But I love him to bits.' She kissed the baby on the forehead and pulled him close to her. 'John's given me a great chance to come back and do this job. Few men would do what he's doing, letting me continue my career.'

'No, you're right there. He's a good man,' said Macleod.

'So are you, and you're going to have to take this little one occasionally and give him a break.'

'Why can't you give him a break?' said Macleod.

'Well, you've left me with this family here to sort out,' said Hope. The telephone rang, and Macleod answered it. He put the phone down about ten seconds later.

'You got something,' said Hope, looking at his anxious face.

'No, that was Tanya. Upstairs wants me to talk about budgets in five minutes' time.'

'I'd better let you go then.'

'No, stuff them. I haven't seen you in a while. I haven't seen this little one. Stay.' He picked up the phone again. 'Tanya, tell them I'm unavailable. I've got a problem I need to look at immediately. Yes, urgent. Don't tell them what it is. Just say urgent. I'll deal with them later.'

He looked across at Hope and smiled. 'Yes, Tanya, bring some coffee in.'

'You're serious,' said Hope. 'You really are serious.'

'Yes,' said Macleod, 'and I've never felt better.'

Read on to discover the Patrick Smythe series!

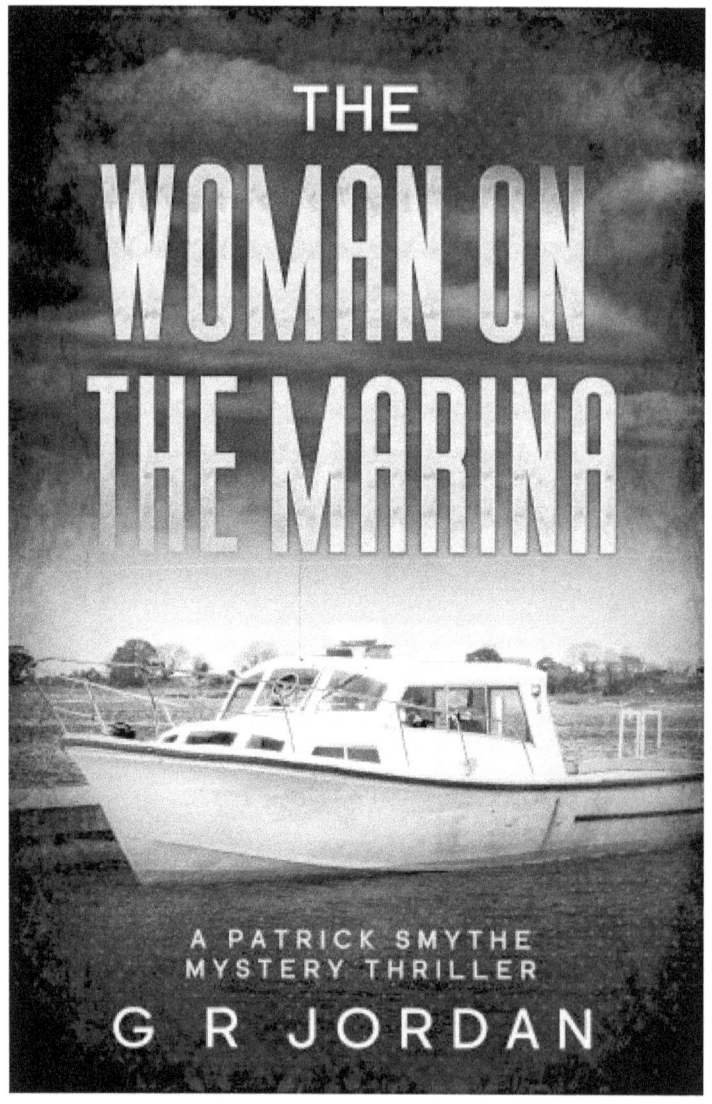

THE
WOMAN ON
THE MARINA

A PATRICK SMYTHE
MYSTERY THRILLER

G R JORDAN

Patrick Smythe is a former Northern Irish policeman who after suffering an amputation after a bomb blast, takes to the sea between the west coast of Scotland and his homeland to ply his trade as a private investigator. Join Paddy as he tries to work to his own ethics while knowing how to bend the rules he once enforced. Working from his beloved motorboat 'Craigantlet', Paddy decides to rescue a drug mule in this short story from the pen of G R Jordan.

Join G R Jordan's monthly newsletter about forthcoming releases and special writings for his tribe of avid readers and then receive your free Patrick Smythe short story.

Go to https://bit.ly/PatrickSmythe for your Patrick Smythe journey to start

About the Author

GR Jordan is a self-published author who finally decided at forty that in order to have an enjoyable lifestyle, his creative beast within would have to be unleashed. His books mirror that conflict in life where acts of decency contend with self-promotion, goodness stares in horror at evil, and kindness blindsides us when we at our worst. Corrupting our world with his parade of wondrous and horrific characters, he highlights everyday tensions with fresh eyes whilst taking his methodical, intelligent mainstays on a roller-coaster ride of dilemmas, all the while suffering the banter of their provocative sidekicks.

A graduate of Loughborough University where he masqueraded as a chemical engineer but ultimately played American football, Gary had worked at changing the shape of cereal flakes and pulled a pallet truck for a living. Watching vegetables freeze at -40'C was another career highlight and he was also one of the Scottish Highlands "blind" air traffic controllers.

These days he has graduated to answering a telephone to people in trouble before telephoning other people to sort it out.

Having flirted with most places in the UK, he is now based in the Isle of Lewis in Scotland where his free time is spent between raising a young family with his wife, writing, figuring out how to work a loom and caring for a small flock of chickens. Luckily, his writing is influenced by his varied work and life experience as the chickens have not been the poetical inspiration he had hoped for!

You can connect with me on:
🌐 https://grjordan.com
📘 https://facebook.com/carpetlessleprechaun

Subscribe to my newsletter:
✉ https://bit.ly/PatrickSmythe

Also by G R Jordan

G R Jordan writes across multiple genres including crime, dark and action adventure fantasy, feel good fantasy, mystery thriller and horror fantasy. Below is a selection of his work. Whilst all books are available across online stores, signed copies are available at his personal shop.

Murder on the Quiet (Highlands & Islands Detective Book 49)

https://grjordan.com/product/murder-on-the-quiet

A new retreat on a remote Scottish island. Illness removes a family from scheduled activities not to be seen again. Can new mother DI Hope McGrath protect her own family and discover the real reason for the resort's creation?

Following the birth of her child in tumultuous circumstances, Hope McGrath is surprised to win a family retreat for her newly expanded family. With partner John and new child Ian, Hope partakes in the first weeks of a resort created on the island of Boreray, part of the St Kilda archipelago. While revelling in the plush and unusual surroundings, a family man succumbs to illness and subsequently disappear from activities. When Hope tries to discover further details regarding the situation, she is fobbed off and her detective's instincts come to the fore. Amongst a barrage of polite obstruction, the detective inspector must use her guile and wit to reveal the link between the guests and who made a haven for murder.

There's nothing as dangerous as a bit of relaxation!

Kirsten Stewart Thrillers
https://grjordan.com/product/a-shot-at-democracy

Join Kirsten Stewart on a shadowy ride through the underbelly of the Highlands of Scotland where among the beauty and splendour of the majestic landscape lies corruption and intrigue to match any city. From murders to extortion, missing children to criminals operating above the law, the Highland former detective must learn a tougher edge to her work as she puts her own life on the line to protect those who cannot defend themselves.

Having left her beloved murder investigation team far behind, Kirsten has to battle personal tragedy and loss while adapting to a whole new way of executing her duties where your mistakes are your own. As Kirsten comes to terms with working with the new team, she often operates as the groups solo field agent, placing herself in danger and trouble to rescue those caught on the dark side of life. With action packed scenes and tense scenarios of murder and greed, the Kirsten Stewart thrillers will have you turning page after page to see your favourite Scottish lass home!

There's life after Macleod, but a whole new world of death!

Jac's Revenge (A Jac Moonshine Thriller #1)

https://grjordan.com/product/jacs-revenge

An unexpected hit makes Debbie a widow. The attention of her man's killer spawns a brutal yet classy alter ego. But how far can you play the game before it takes over your life?

All her life, Debbie Parlor lived in her man's shadow, knowing his work was never truly honest. She turned her head from news stories and rumours. But when he was disposed of for his smile to placate a rival crime lord, Jac Moonshine was born. And when Debbie is paid compensation for her loss like her car was written off, Jac decides that enough is enough.

Get on board with this tongue-in-cheek revenge thriller that will make you question how far you would go to avenge a loved one, and how much you would enjoy it!

A Giant Killing (Siobhan Duffy Mysteries #1)

https://grjordan.com/product/a-giant-killing

A body lies on the Giant's boot. Discord, as the master of secrets has been found. Can former spy Siobhan Duffy find the killer before they execute her former colleagues?

When retired operative Siobhan Duffy sees the killing of her former master in the paper, her unease sends her down a path of discovery and fear. Aided by her young housekeeper and scruff of a gardener, Siobhan begins a quest to discover the reason for her spy boss' death and unravels a can of worms today's masters would rather keep closed. But in a world of secrets, the difference between revenge and simple, if brutal, housekeeping becomes the hardest truth to know.

The past is a child who never leaves home!

www.ingramcontent.com/pod-product-compliance
Ingram Content Group UK Ltd.
Pitfield, Milton Keynes, MK11 3LW, UK
UKHW010809191025
464082UK00001B/6